# ANGELS

## A DARK DRABBLES ANTHOLOGY

Compiled & Edited by D Kershaw

Also available from Black Hare Press


DARK DRABBLES ANTHOLOGIES


WORLDS
MONSTERS
BEYOND
UNRAVEL

A catalogue record for this
book is available from the
National Library of Australia

ISBN 978-1-925809-14-5

Cover design by Dawn Burdett
Formatting by Ben Thomas

Come to me when grief is over,
When the tired eyes,
Seek thy cloudy wings to cover
Close their burning skies.

Come to me when tears have dwindled
Into drops of dew,
When the sighs like sobs re-kindled
Are but deep and few.

Hold me like a crooning mother,
Heal me of the smart;
All mine anguish let me smother
In thy brooding heart.

- Duncan Campbell Scott, "Angel"

# Table of Contents

# Foreword

Angels. Those benevolent celestial beings who guard and guide us, protect and collect us.

The legends and myths fascinate us, the beauty astounds us, but are these seraphs mere fantasia—moralistic fairy tales meant to teach us life lessons, help us be good citizens—or should we fear the ebon wings, bathe in the light of the golden halos… hedge our bets?

Whether you fear them or revere them, or see them as flights of fantasy, we hope you enjoy these tiny tales of blasphemy and piety by accomplished authors from all over the world, collated for your divine delectation.

Love and kisses
D. Kershaw & Ben Thomas
Black Hare Press

# Sofia
by Ximena Escobar

Beautiful is you, my sunshine, my angel. Carry me over the ruins of my crushed dreams, over the lovers lost, the friends I failed to save. The strangers I failed to see, the hugs I failed to give, the words I didn't know to choose because pain sometimes twirls itself into wrong tongue shapes. Fly me over the wounds I inflicted, because I was wounded. Carry me, as you do, with your beautiful smile like wings. Elevate me to the height of loving you, with every breath I take filling my chest of you; my joy, my pride, my everything.

*Ximena Escobar is an emerging author of literary fiction and poetry. Originally from Chile, she is the author of a translation into Spanish of the Broadway Musical "The Wizard of Oz", and of an original adaptation of the same, "Navidad en Oz". Clarendon House Publications published her first short story in the UK, "The Persistence of Memory", and Literally Stories her first online publication with "The Green Light". She has since had several acceptances from other publishers and is working very hard exploring new exciting avenues in her writing.*
*She lives in Nottingham with her family.*
*Facebook: Ximenautora*

# Everything
## by Jacob Baugher

When I was dying from brain cancer, Michael came to visit me. One second, I was alone in the hospital, watching the game. The next, he sat on my bedside sipping coffee, angelic wings folded.

"That quarterback is gonna get injured."

"Christ, you have to stop doing that."

"I will if you stop saying 'Christ.'"

Silence fell. Michael finished his coffee and asked if I was ready.

"Not yet."

"Are you afraid?"

"No. There's one more thing I have to see."

I cradled my first grandson 6 months later.

"Michael," I whispered. I kissed Ben's forehead. "Now I've seen everything."

*Jacob Baugher teaches Creative Writing at Franciscan University of Steubenville. When he's not teaching or coaching the track team, he can be found in the Cuyahoga Valley hiking with his wife and son or brewing beer on his front porch. He's received honourable mentions for his work in the Writers of the Future contest and he co-edits a series of Fantasy and Science Fiction anthologies titled Continuum.*

# Weeping Angel
## by D.M. Burdett

Here I sit upon on my charge's final resting place; a stone effigy, weeping tears for this child, for her suffering. This is my eternal fate; for my failures will haunt me for all time. I shall cry silently forever in sadness and desolation.

But I wait.

For when he comes—and he *will* come—revenge will be mine. Her father's eyes will gaze upon me and I will torment his soul for the suffering he's inflicted; he will writhe in my anger, suffocate in my hatred, fester in my rage.

And if he looks away, I will devour him.

*D.M. Burdett initially roamed as an army brat, but now lives in Australia where she spends her days avoiding drop bears and killer spiders. She has published a Sci-Fi series, has short stories in various anthologies, and has published two children's series. She is currently working on the first book in a dystopian series.*
*Website: www.dmburdett.com*
*Facebook: DMBurdett*

# Everybody Loves Dean Winchester
## by Shelly Jarvis

I didn't *mean* to fall. Not like you think, anyway.

Hell, most of us didn't. We were just tired and bored, ready for something else. Watching the old man fawn over his precious humans was a real downer.

So, we split. We weren't looking for trouble, but it found us, man. Now we're the bad guys in the stories. Literally, all of them. You watch *Buffy the Vampire Slayer*? How 'bout *Supernatural*? I'm a *Dean* guy myself.

The point is, we're not all bad. I can prove it. Gimme your soul for a sec. I promise it won't hurt. Much.

*Shelly Jarvis is a speculative fiction author from West Virginia, US. She found a life-long love of sci-fi and fantasy in the 3rd grade when she found Madeleine L'Engle's "A Wrinkle in Time." Shelly is an avid reader, a Whovian, the ideal viewer of dog rescue videos, and undoubtedly Ravenclaw. She currently has two YA sci-fi books available for purchase on Amazon.*
*Website: www.ShellyJarvis.com*

# Gentle Black Wings
## by Lynne Lumsden Green

The Angel of Death is deeply in love with the Angel of Life; and he returns her love. Contrary to what mortals might think, Death is never unfair or cruel; she plays no part in the actual process of dying. Dying wreaks havoc on the systems of Life and breaks the bonds between body and soul. Death is the full stop at the end of a sentence.

Death has gentle black wings. As Life releases you into the care of Death, she will carry away as softly and silently as an owl. You're a love poem from Life to Death.

*Lynne Lumsden Green has twin bachelor's degrees in both Science and the Arts, giving her the balance between rationality and creativity. She spent fifteen years as the Science Queen for HarperCollins Voyager Online and has written science articles for other online magazines. Currently, she captains the Writing Race for the Australian Writers Marketplace on Facebook. She has had speculative fiction flash fiction and short stories published in anthologies and websites.*
*Website: cogpunksteamscribe.wordpress.com*

# The Fallen Angel of Permission
## by Jefferson Retallack

Serenity, Impasse, Exuberance, and I took on new names. We saw the light for what it was. The angels would label us demons. But we're the same as them, only better.

Our advantage?

Free will.

Reborn, we had ended the Angel of Grief's stranglehold over the mortal world, rending him into five fragments.

His left arm, Denial, sought retribution. He actually thought he'd won when the glacier entombed us upon our flight from heaven.

I called forth a fire to my palms, hotter than any ever witnessed, and crashed through the ice, evaporating both it and Denial.

My name?

Permission.

*Jefferson Retallack is an Australian writer of speculative fiction. He is based in Adelaide. His work draws influence from linguistic science fiction, the new weird and Australia's big things. Outside of the literary world, he skateboards on the weekends and spends afternoons on the beach with his partner, their son, and their Pomeranian, Tofu.*
*Website: jwretallack.wordpress.com*
*Twitter: @JWRetallack*

# The Fallen Angel of Serenity
by Jefferson Retallack

The Angel of Grief now vanquished, his right arm, Anger, seized the opportunity to insight discord among our following.

With mortals no longer held back following the experience of loss, Anger redoubled the earthly efforts of the Angels.

Inequality and inhumanity ran rampant. Acts of terror became daily occurrences. The fallen Angel of Serenity could not abide such a plague.

Grief had impeded creativity. With his limitation eliminated, Serenity was free to work his magic. A wave of passion flooded the earth, tweaking Anger's efforts. The incensed now made art, love where once was war.

Anger survived, powerless.

Serenity thrived.

*Jefferson Retallack is an Australian writer of speculative fiction. He is based in Adelaide. His work draws influence from linguistic science fiction, the new weird and Australia's big things. Outside of the literary world, he skateboards on the weekends and spends afternoons on the beach with his partner, their son, and their Pomeranian, Tofu.*
*Website: jwretallack.wordpress.com*
*Twitter: @JWRetallack*

# The Fallen Angel of Impasse
by Jefferson Retallack

The severed left leg of the Angel of Grief, Bargaining, was quick to pit us against one another.

Serenity and Exuberance had to prevent a flood from silencing a sleeping town, or redirect a parade from dancing into a sinkhole. No time for both.

Impasse and myself, Permission, were tasked with saving either Vatican City or Jerusalem from erasure by earthquake.

The Angel of Bargaining had counted on us to be limited by our free will. But Impasse's stoicism conceded no power to him.

Impasse demanded we make no decision. Some harm now preventing more in the future.

Bargaining withered.

*Jefferson Retallack* *is an Australian writer of speculative fiction. He is based in Adelaide. His work draws influence from linguistic science fiction, the new weird and Australia's big things. Outside of the literary world, he skateboards on the weekends and spends afternoons on the beach with his partner, their son, and their Pomeranian, Tofu.*
*Website: jwretallack.wordpress.com*
*Twitter: @JWRetallack*

# The Fallen Angel of Exuberance
## by Jefferson Retallack

We, the fallen angels who slayed the Angel of Grief, still suffered two avengers upon reaching Earth.

Depression, the penultimate reprover and right leg of Grief's corpse, had risked abandoning Heaven to put a stop to our plans.

He blanketed the world with a network of instant gratification and paranoia. People lost the ability to cultivate community. Their worship grew private, losing its potency.

All looked lost.

But Exuberance could not be suppressed. He taught the people to repurpose Depression's labyrinth of isolation. Now they tend the virtuous, distance no barrier.

Exuberance, Impasse, Serenity, and I were nearly, truly free.

*Jefferson Retallack is an Australian writer of speculative fiction. He is based in Adelaide. His work draws influence from linguistic science fiction, the new weird and Australia's big things. Outside of the literary world, he skateboards on the weekends and spends afternoons on the beach with his partner, their son, and their Pomeranian, Tofu.*
*Website: jwretallack.wordpress.com*
*Twitter: @JWRetallack*

# The Falling Angel of Acceptance
## by Jefferson Retallack

The Angel of Grief communed with us once we'd moved beyond the Earth's crust to its centre.

"We've defeated your four retaliators, Grief."

"Grief is no longer. Acceptance remains."

"You cannot restore our station."

The Angel of Acceptance materialised in our inferno. Its tangled mass of flesh writhed before us—a terrible sight, made worse by the four limbs we had effaced.

"No. But I can join you."

And so, the Angel of Acceptance made us—Exuberance, Impasse, Serenity, and Permission—its new limbs. We could not deny it, grow angry, bargain, nor vow depression to escape this new Hell.

*Jefferson Retallack is an Australian writer of speculative fiction. He is based in Adelaide. His work draws influence from linguistic science fiction, the new weird and Australia's big things. Outside of the literary world, he skateboards on the weekends and spends afternoons on the beach with his partner, their son, and their Pomeranian, Tofu.*
*Website: jwretallack.wordpress.com*
*Twitter: @JWRetallack*

# Brothers
## by E.L. Giles

"Shouldn't we take action?" Aquila asked distressfully.

"No," retorted Cassius, repulsion permeating his voice. He leaned over the edge of the monolith on which he and Aquila were seated. His seraphic eyes were cold as he watched the bloody war that ravaged Earth.

"Shouldn't we protect our human brothers?" said Aquila, offended, gripping his golden spear firmly. He was about to jump off the marble monolith.

"You are young, Aquila. One day, you will realise that our brothers are simply hopeless. They are violent, hateful, and unreliable."

"You speak like Lucifer!" shouted Aquila, pointing a finger at Cassius.

"So what?"

*E.L. Giles is a dreamer, passionate about art, a restless worker and a bit of a weird human. He started his artistic journey as a music composer until the need to put his thoughts and stories down on paper grew too strong for him to resist it any longer. He lives in the French Province of Quebec, Canada, with his girlfriend and two boys.*
*Facebook: elgilesauthor*
*Website: www.elgilesauthor.com*

# The Eternal Conflict
## by Stuart Conover

The struggle between good and evil had gone on as long as Rayzon remembered.

Gods pitted one side against the other in an eternal war.

They didn't even know what they were fighting for.

The battle was long fought as his men died around him.

Finally, Rayzon was the last one standing.

It wasn't long until he too fell.

Eyed trapped wide open he knew it would all begin again soon.

His warriors and their sworn enemies resurrected.

In the sky above, the mysterious signal which signified a brief halt of conflict started to blink.

"Enter 25 Cents To Play."

*Stuart Conover is a father, husband, rescue dog owner, published author, blogger, journalist, horror enthusiast, comic book geek, science fiction junkie, and IT professional. With all of that to cram in daily, we have no idea if or when he sleeps or how he gets writing done! (We suspect it has to do with having evil clones.) Stuart is a Chicago native and runs the author resource Horror Tree.*

# Prisoner in Stone
## by George Nikolopoulos

The winged bull watched the world through stone eyes.

He recalled the day of his binding, surrounded by Babylonian priests. "Pazuzu, vile Demon of the Air," they chanted, "long have we suffered your malevolence. You shall be encased in stone forever."

Countless centuries passed. Powerless, forgotten, Pazuzu languished in his stony prison.

Today, a huge mob of angry men assembled around him. "We'll destroy the idols of the false gods," they cried. As they struck the statue with their hammers, cracks appeared on its surface.

Pazuzu flexed his muscles, looking at the mob. Time to break free. Time to feed.

*George Nikolopoulos is a speculative fiction writer from Athens, Greece, and a member of Codex Writers' Group. His short stories have been published in over 60 magazines and anthologies including Galaxy's Edge, Nature, Daily Science Fiction, Factor Four, Grievous Angel, Best Vegan SFF, and The Year's Best Military & Adventure SF.*
*Website: georgenikolopoulos.wordpress.com*
*Twitter: @g_nikolop*

# The Limbo Lounge
## by Shawn M. Klimek

Leaving his white wings on the hook near the door, Pasty strode up to the bar and took the empty stool beside Smudgy.

The bartender loomed expectantly.

Aiming a thumb, Pasty said, "I'll have the opposite of what he's having."

The bartender nodded and retreated.

Smudgy blew smoke at Pasty, who waved it away.

"You shouldn't smoke," Pasty complained.

"It's my best natural feature," said Smudgy.

The bartender placed a glass of whiskey in front of him.

Confused, he demanded, "How is this the opposite of what he's drinking?"

The bartender turned up a palm and explained, "His was free."

*Shawn M. Klimek is a writer whose other recent anthologies include: "Full Metal Horror 2", by Zombie Pirate Publishing, "Organic Ink" by Dragon Soul Press, "Grumpy Old Gods (Vols. 1 & 2)" by Stormdance Publications, and soon, "Blaze: Inner Circle Writer's Group Flash Fiction Anthology 2019."*
*Website: jotinthedark.blogspot.com*
*Facebook: shawnmklimekauthor*

# Angel vs Society
## by Becky Benishek

The battle was within her; no holy war, was this.

She'd established her personal laws before she knew better, enshrouded in "supposed to," "mustn't," and "should." The intoxication of conforming gladly took her in its snare, and demon teeth bestowed approbation.

The angel within spoke of her true nature, her gifts, her own path. Confused, she ran instead to people happy to keep her confined.

But her pesky true nature kept trying to break free, until finally it did.

Fallen now, bleeding, dropped by the disgust of false friends. Who was she now?

Herself.

And the angel within her soared.

*Becky Benishek is the author of the children's books "The Squeezor is Coming!", "What's At the End of Your Nose?", "Dr. Guinea Pig George," and "Hush, Mouse!" She loves to create stories that help children believe in themselves and find the magic in ordinary things. Becky also manages online communities that connect people with resources to help people with special needs thrive. She has an extensive Lego collection, a working Commodore 64, and a tendency to stick googly eyes on objects minding their own business. Becky is married with guinea pigs.*
*Website: beckybenishek.com*
*Amazon: www.amazon.com/author/beckybenishek*

# Something Better
## by Gabriella Balcom

"Scampers, quit it!" Susan fussed.

But the kitten leapt onto her plate again before hiding.

Waking later, Scampers smelled smoke and found Susan in bed. She didn't budge when he nosed her and meowed, so he bit her. She roused, coughing.

He pawed Daisy next. The dog staggered to her feet, but the kitten swayed on his.

When firemen arrived, only Susan and Daisy were outside.

***

Scampers woke in heaven. "Is my family okay?" he asked.

"You saved them," God replied.

"I didn't get nine lives."

"You're getting something better."

Wide-eyed, Scampers admired his wings. "Me? An angel?"

God smiled.

*Gabriella Balcom* lives in Texas with her family, loves reading and writing, and thinks she was born with a book in her hands. She works in a mental health field, and writes fantasy, horror/thriller, romance, children's stories, and sci-fi. She likes travelling, music, good shows, photography, history, interesting tales, and animals. Gabriella says she's a sucker for a great story and loves forests, mountains, and back roads which might lead who knows where. She has a weakness for lasagne, garlic bread, tacos, cheese, and chocolate, but not necessarily in that order.
Facebook: GabriellaBalcom.lonestarauthor

# A Tarnished Halo
## by Jo Seysener

Helio held her head high, wings stretched to their fullest as she soared away from the dank cave. Her wrists stung where the manacles had rested.

Pretending she'd escaped, not craving her own humiliation.

She shimmered, disappearing from the demon's sight. As she entered the Void, her neck slid down between her shoulder blades, tips of her wings drooping.

*Ashamed.*

Seeing herself exposed, feathers singed, dangling between the chains—it gave her power. Even as she let his claws scour her, stroking her skin, her purity bleeding onto the unconsecrated floor. Releasing her to Save.

But never to Fall.

*Jo Seysener is a mum of three crazies, a scatter of chickens, a decrepit kelpie and a rambunctious GSD. She lives with her husband near Brisbane, Australia. When she is not exposing her kids to cult story books from her childhood, she can be found in the kitchen experimenting with new flavours and pairings. She adores alpacas.*
*Facebook: joseysener*
*Website: www.joseysener.com*

# Unending Love
## by Kyle Harrison

Last night I met the Grim Reaper; he said he'd change my life.

He told me I would be happy if first I left my wife.


I told him that I did not care what sort of games he played.

Because I love her dearly, so home's where I stayed.


He warned me not to be so sure.

To make sure my love was pure.


I hastened home, to seek her smile.

To stay in her arms, dream awhile.


"Do you love me?" I asked, awaiting the response she gave.

But the dead can never answer from beyond the grave.


*Kyle Harrison is a successfully published short story horror novelist and has been in over 6 anthologies and managed 3 anthologies himself. He has also been a project manager for Kickstarters and served as a mentor for other aspiring writers.*

# Angel of the Outback
## by John H. Dromey

Imagine the immense relief of a motorist stranded by mechanical problems on a long, lonely stretch of highway when a dusty utility vehicle comes into view and pulls up alongside the stalled auto.

Even better, the newcomer has a suitable spare part in the cargo tray of his ute. He makes the repair and is amply rewarded.

Austin Killy was no angel in disguise. He was more of a bird of prey or a vulture with an accomplice who sabotaged selected vehicles in petrol stations or car parks.

The highway patrol clipped Austin's wings and put him in a cage.

*John H. Dromey was born in northeast Missouri, USA. He enjoys reading—mysteries in particular—and writing in a variety of genres. He's had short fiction published in Alfred Hitchcock's Mystery Magazine, Martian Magazine, Stupefying Stories Showcase, Thriller Magazine, Unfit Magazine, and elsewhere, as well as in a number of anthologies, including Chilling Horror Short Stories (Flame Tree Publishing, 2015).*

# Alice's Cherub
## by J.D. Bell

Howls and curses erupted from the man's mouth. Alice hated the way he treated her mother. She wanted her father back. Every night since his death, she prayed he would return to her.

A young spirit, a winged cherub, came one night. "Have faith, Alice. Your father sent me to protect you and your mother."

Working off an anonymous tip, the police arrested the man on a series of assault charges. As they lead him away, Alice saw the cherub appear and smile at her. Then she heard her father speak through the cherub. "I will always protect you, Alice."

*J.D. Bell is an award-winning, internationally published, author of flash fiction and short stories. He recently retired from the world of writing advertising copy and is now enjoying the universe of creative fiction.*
*Facebook: jim.writes.stories*
*Twitter: @JimBell58*

# The Root of Ebon Wings
## by Terry Miller

Jocelyn cut off her wings, her scabbed shoulder blades revealed. *I'm not worthy of being an angel*, she thought.

"Forgive me, Father," she cried. "I am unworthy."

The Father was silent.

Out of the darkness a voice whispered, "Why have you defiled yourself so?"

A tear disturbed the puddle below.

"Who are you?" the angel inquired.

"I am the root of ebon wings."

"Ebon wings?"

"I am."

"I don't understand."

The scabs ached as black feathers broke through until new wings stretched and fluttered.

"Now fly with me."

Jocelyn soared into the darkness, its mysteries whispered to her attentive ears.

***Terry Miller*** *is an author and 2017 Rhysling Award-nominated poet residing in Portsmouth, OH, USA. He has self-published a dark poetry collection on Amazon and one short story to date. His work has also appeared in Sanitarium, Devolution Z, Jitter Press, Poetry Quarterly, O Unholy Night in Deathlehem, and the 2017 Rhysling Anthology from the Science Fiction and Fantasy Poetry Association.*
*Facebook: tmiller2015*

# Seraphin
## by Cecelia Hopkins-Drewer

Zafin nursed her broken wing. Everywhere she looked, evil seemed to be overcoming good. One dark angel was causing floods across half of the globe, while another was causing fire, and the war angel was shooting bolts all over the place.

"Come with me," it was a dark angel. "I'm tired of the fighting—I just want to go somewhere and live in peace!"

"Never!" Zafin exclaimed. She pushed the evil angel so that it fell off the cloud, spinning and struggling to regain control in the sparse atmosphere.

Then she turned back to the Earth. Evil was definitely winning.

*Cecelia Hopkins-Drewer is a speculative fiction writer, poet and scholar, who lives in Adelaide, South Australia. She has also written a Masters paper on H.P. Lovecraft, and a teenage vampire series that commences with "Mystic Evermore". Her science fiction poetry has been published in "The Mentor" a fanzine edited by Ron Clarke.*
*Amazon: amazon.com/Cecelia-Hopkins-Drewer/e/B071G968NM*

# Allied Defence
by William J. Joel

"General? No slight intended, but you *do* realise that nuclear weapons will have no effect on demons?"

General Montague looked up from the report he'd been reading.

"And just who in God's name are you, son?"

I smiled. In God's name. Yes, very appropriate. I gave him a quick salute.

"Name's Zebadiah, sir. Archangel Zebadiah, of God's Fourth Battalion."

He placed the report on the table. Then he laughed. "Archangel? God's battalion?"

"Fourth Battalion," I replied.

General Montague moved his face within an inch of mine.

"Sergeant? Get this asshole outta here!"

You can't teach an old human new tricks.

*All things are connected. That's the premise of what **William J. Joel** does. Each of Mr. Joel's interests informs each other. Mr. Joel has been teaching computer science since 1983 and has been a poet even longer. His poems have appeared in Chronogram, Common Ground Review, and Gravel Magazine.*
*Website: www.aniprof.com*

# Angels of Destruction
## by C.L. Williams

Twins Leonardo and Cyrus always fought, not knowing this would one day be a prophecy. As they got older, tensions only grew. No one knew how much hatred the brothers truly had for one another until it was too late. One day, the soothsayer entered the village to try to bring peace to the brothers. She felt the aura from them and noticed something no one else saw. One, an angel of creation, the other was an angel of destruction. One day, while fighting, Leonardo sprouted bright white wings, Cyrus two flaming black wings. They are the angels of destruction.

*C.L. Williams is an independent author from central Virginia. He has written eight poetry books, four novellas, one novel, and a contributor to multiple anthologies, with the most recent appearance being an all-ages anthology titled Temoli from Thazbook. His most recent poetry book, The Paradox Complex, features the poem "Sad Crying Clown" that is now a video on YouTube directed by Matthew Mark Hunter of MMH Productions. C.L. Williams is currently working on his first sci-fi book, an all-ages book titled Novo: Away from Earth. When not writing, C.L. Williams is reading and sharing the work of other independent authors.*
*Facebook: writer434*
*Twitter: @writer_434*

# Silence
## by K.T. Tate

They appeared instantly, as if suddenly materialising out of our collective blind spot. Gigantic beings of inconceivable design, standing there like eldritch statues. Their forms barely humanoid, their features a mockery of nature, all faceless.

We panicked, probed, took sides and yet they did nothing.

Until the seventh day.

A single celestial note rang out, obliterating all sound, calling them to action. We heard nothing as our blood splattered the streets. Screams of pain and prayers for salvation were lost to the noiseless catastrophe. Whether angels or demons they brought the end. And the world of men fell in silence.

*K.T. Tate lives in Cambridgeshire in the UK. She writes mainly weird fiction, cosmic horror and strange monster stories.*
*Website: eldritchhollow.wordpress.com*
*Tumblr: eldritch-hollow.tumblr.com*

# The Last Mission
## by E.L. Giles

"Where will you go when I will die?" asked the old man. His angel stared at him.

"My mission will be over," she answered sadly. Frowning, she looked around at the desolate and barren land, rendered unhabitable by mankind, and then back at the old man, the very last man on Earth.

"So, you will die too?" asked the old man. A tear rolled down his cheek. She smiled.

"I will," she answered simply. "There is nothing else for me here. Nothing at all for us angels. We are doomed to extinction."

"I'm sorry," said the old man.

"Me too."

*E.L. Giles is a dreamer, passionate about art, a restless worker and a bit of a weird human. He started his artistic journey as a music composer until the need to put his thoughts and stories down on paper grew too strong for him to resist it any longer. He lives in the French Province of Quebec, Canada, with his girlfriend and two boys.*
*Facebook: elgilesauthor*
*Website: www.elgilesauthor.com*

# Angelica
## by Vonnie Winslow Crist

"To ward off disease, chew the seeds of Angelica Archangelica, the herb of angels," read Hildy from her physick book. "Though illness is not your problem, Angelica will help."

Pasha nodded.

"Angelica buds, harvested at Michaelmas, tied in a pouch, and placed beneath your pillow while praying to the Archangel Michael should undo the spell."

"A sorcerer!" gasped Pasha.

"Yes," said Hildy as she handed Pasha a mug of Angelica root juice. "First, drink this, then follow my instructions exactly."

Once Pasha had departed, Hildy shrugged off her wisewoman guise. In angel garb, she went to deal with the sorcerer.

*Vonnie Winslow Crist is author of The Enchanted Dagger, Owl Light, The Greener Forest, Murder on Marawa Prime, and other award-winning books. Her fiction is included in "Amazing Stories," "Cast of Wonders," "Outposts of Beyond," Killing It Softly 2, Defending the Future - Dogs of War, Midnight Masquerade, Chaos of Hard Clay, and elsewhere. A cloverhand who has found so many four-leafed clovers she keeps them in jars, Vonnie strives to celebrate the power of myth in her writing.*
*Website: www.vonniewinslowcrist.com*

# Music
## by D.M. Burdett

My family surrounds me; they are but a dim glow, a quiet, babbling brook of muted sound.

I only hear the harps.

Ethereal music fills my consciousness. White and gold fills my vision.

I smile, because now I *know* what will become of me; these angelic beings will carry me to Heaven.

I see a flash of ebon, feel a breath's touch of feathers.

I turn my beaming, reverent face. "Is it time?"

With a flick of the wrist, the conductor—this magnificent dark angel—silences the orchestra.

The room darkens, and fires rage.

"Oh, yes." Lucifer whispers, eyes twinkling.

*D.M. Burdett initially roamed as an army brat, but now lives in Australia where she spends her days avoiding drop bears and killer spiders. She has published a Sci-Fi series, has short stories in various anthologies, and has published two children's series. She is currently working on the first book in a dystopian series.*
*Website: www.dmburdett.com*
*Facebook: DMBurdett*

# God is Actually a Troll
## by Jimmy Zarecky

Everyone thinks the good guys are lame, but I'll take blazing swords over horns and hellfire any eternity.

Gabriel sent me Below to talk to Lucifer. I call him Lucy to piss him off. Lava shoots out from his bat-ears on his bat-face. He's got a throne of black obsidian and a hall of black obsidian. A white cat sits on his lap. Lucy really got into the Bond villain thing.

I float on falcon wings. The snakeskin floor writhes. Somewhere Beyond, telemarketers scream their recorded agony.

"What?" Lucy snaps.

"Gabriel wanted to tell you…"

"Yes?"

"That you a bitch."

*Jimmy Zarecky lives in a suburb of Baltimore, MD, where his grandparents settled in 1925 after emigrating from then-Czechoslovakia. In his free time, he writes failed novels and works in a craft coffee shop. Mark Hamill once liked one of his tweets.*

# Family Ties
## by Alanah Andrews

"I don't wanna do it." Christine stamped her foot, shuddering the Earth.

"It's in your blood," said her father.

"I don't care. I'm not interested in—" she spread her hands "—in any of this."

"Guardian angel, Christmas tree angel, or statue? You choose."

"I don't wanna be any sort of angel." Christine flew high into the air, turned gracefully, and plummeted into the ground.

Shockwave. Screams. Collapsed buildings.

Then silence.

"Congratulations," said her father sadly, surveying the devastation. "You got what you wanted."

"I didn't—"

"Now, do you want to cut off your wings, or shall I?"

*Alanah Andrews* *writes speculative fiction and spends far too much time debating whether 1984 or The Handmaid's Tale are most representative of our future. Her YA dystopian novel about a future where emotions are forbidden, Eve of Eridu, was released in 2018. She has also had several short stories published in a range of different places. When she's not writing, Alanah runs the Australian Speculative Fiction group, teaches high school English, and attempts to raise two children. She has a husky, a pony, a blue-tongue lizard, and dreams of travelling Australia in a bus.*
*Website: www.alanahandrews.com*
*Facebook: alanahandrewsauthor*

# The Telekinetic Con-Demon
## by Jacob Baugher

Sometimes, I use telekinesis to con men at Frank's Tavern. I'd pluck an ice cube out of a Fireball, float it down to the bar.

What? Demons have horns. Men like breasts and exotic women.

I try it on Teddy, he says, "Stop effin off."

Religious guys don't swear. He buys me an Old-fashioned.

We're together for a while but, apparently, I 'lead him into sin.'

He seemed to like it.

The note on my dresser says, "Mara, had fun, but I hate myself with you."

The self-righteous fool. I fling his car into a wormhole. Boring, my demonic ass.

*Jacob Baugher teaches Creative Writing at Franciscan University of Steubenville. When he's not teaching or coaching the track team, he can be found in the Cuyahoga Valley hiking with his wife and son or brewing beer on his front porch. He's received honourable mentions for his work in the Writers of the Future contest and he co-edits a series of Fantasy and Science Fiction anthologies titled Continuum.*

# The Seventh Seal
## by Zoey Xolton

The archangel Michael brought the golden trumpet to his lips, sounding the End of Days. Now was the time of Revelations. The Son of God opened four of the Seven Sacred Seals, parting the veil and unleashing the Four Horsemen; Conquest, War, Famine and Death. They rode forth across the world on stallions of white, red, pale and black.

The Son opened the fifth seal and the people cried out, "How long should we suffer?" And so, He opened the sixth. The earth quaked, the seas rose, great comets fell, and fires burned.

The seventh seal would herald the Rapture.

*Zoey Xolton is an Australian Speculative Fiction writer, primarily of Dark Fantasy, Paranormal Romance and Horror. She is also a proud mother of two and is married to her soul mate. Outside of her family, writing is her greatest passion. She is especially fond of short fiction and is working on releasing her own themed collections in future.*
*Website: www.zoeyxolton.com*

# A Hard Season
## by Stephen Herczeg

The end of a long hard season. The Grand Final. We're away. Even the food vendors hate us.

We've played like crap. Especially me. Nothing's going right. I've barely got a kick.

Late second quarter, twenty points down, racing against my opponent and…*twang!*

It's my quad. I grimace as the physio works on me, but miraculously it starts to feel better. I can go back on.

I look up at the blindingly bright figure before me. Her wings extend to full width.

"We love what you girls are doing out there. Now go win this thing," she says.

*Stephen Herczeg is an IT Geek based in Canberra Australia. He has been writing for over twenty years and has completed a couple of dodgy novels, sixteen feature length screenplays and numerous short stories and scripts. His horror work has featured in Sproutlings, Hells Bells, Below the Stairs, Trickster's Treats #1 and #2, Shades of Santa, Behind the Mask, Beyond the Infinite; The Body Horror Book, Anemone Enemy, Petrified Punks and Beginnings. He has also had numerous Sherlock Holmes stories published through the Belanger Books - Sherlock Holmes anthologies.*

# A Bargain Struck
## by Alexander Pyles

I stood on the shore. Ice water lapped my feet as the boatman emerged. A scythe glimmered, grasped in his skeletal fist. The black smoke of its cloak fanned up like wings and loomed over me.

"And what do you offer?" Its voice radiated out without moving its mouth.

"Myself."

"Come." The boatman's scythe passed over me and I was divided. My body collapsed on the ground. My soul floating above.

My daughter emerged from under Death's mantle, towards the light. She did not look at my body nor my soul. She kept walking, her jaw set and stride confident.

*Alexander Pyles resides in IL with his wife and children. He holds an MA in Philosophy and an MFA in Writing Popular Fiction. His short story chapbook titled, "Milo (01001101 01101001 01101100 01101111)," from Radix Media, is due out fall 2019. His other short fiction has appeared on 101fiction.org, River and South Review, and other venues. Website: www.pylesofbooks.com Twitter: @Pylesofbooks*

# Sisters
by Brian Rosenberger

A family secret kept secret.

A house of lies to protect the family.

Two Sisters. Same mother. Different father. The sisters didn't care. Their fate and ancestry beyond their control. What mattered to the sisters was they were blood. Family. They loved and protected each other. One born of Angel. One born of Mortal. Iris and Dawn. Sisters.

When Iris was raped by their neighbour who they'd both known for years, Dawn was there to comfort her only sister.

Iris was incapable of revenge. Dawn, born of mortal, craved it.

The sisters walked hand in hand at the neighbour's funeral.

*Brian Rosenberger lives in a cellar in Marietta, GA (USA) and writes by the light of captured fireflies. He is the author of As the Worms Turns and three poetry collections. He is also a featured contributor to the Pro-Wrestling literary collection, Three-Way Dance, available from Gimmick Press.*
*Facebook: HeWhoSuffers*

# Angels of the Last Apocalypse
## by Russell Hemmell

Our faces are iron masks, but we are not actors. We wear exoskeletons like carapaces, but we're neither cyborgs nor insects. We're no humans, though, and only in the darkest hours of the night you can look at us in our demonic splendour—translucent and shimmering, lurking in the shadows.

But we're not devils either.

We're the she-spirits of the air, the winds, and the dark-blue sea, born out of the last apocalypse that made of the Earth a desert of stones, and we carve our path into survivors' dreams like a thousand coiling snakes or a sticky rainfall.

***Russell Hemmell** is a French-Italian transplant in Scotland, passionate about astrophysics, history, and speculative fiction. Recent work in Aurelis, The Grievous Angel, Third Flatiron, and others. Codexian & HWA Active Member. Website: earthianhivemind.net Twitter: @SPBianchini*

# Fallen Angel
## by Allen Ashley

How did I get here? I remember stretching out my wings, taking flight…and then nothing. I must have crashed. Failed.

I cannot afford to fail. My task is to stay on guard, to protect my chosen people during this cold, dark season. Be watchful from up on high.

I call for others of my angelic kind to come help me but there are none nearby.

I twitch, flutter, pound my wings…I remain earthbound.

At last, two humans arrive. I feel hands around my body, lifting me back, above the baubles, the lights, to the top of the tree.

*Allen Ashley is a British Fantasy Award winner who works as a creative writing tutor and critical reader in London, UK. His most recent book is as co-editor (with Sarah Doyle) of the anthology "Humanagerie" (Eibonvale Press, 2018) – a collection of short stories and poems exploring human-animal liminality. He has stories due soon in "Shoreline of Infinity", "BFS Horizons" and the NewCon Press anthology "Once Upon A Parsec". He is the founder of the advanced science fiction and fantasy group Clockhouse London Writers.*
*Website: www.allenashley.com*

# One Last Candle
## by Stuart Conover

Lorsep's people didn't follow the old traditions.

Her temple abandoned outside those drowning in misery.

Now, she called her own faith into question.

Yet here she was.

Lighting the candles.

Speaking the prayers.

A natural warrior, she'd never see battle.

Her life wasted in these walls.

The final candle lit, she turned to leave.

Before her, bathed in light was The Silent Majority.

The voice of the Dwarven Gods.

Its mouth opened and Lorsep knew her people were doomed.

She'd accompany the new King to war.

Her people would be broken.

She blacked, knowing her ancestral home was already burning.

*Stuart Conover is a father, husband, rescue dog owner, published author, blogger, journalist, horror enthusiast, comic book geek, science fiction junkie, and IT professional. With all of that to cram in daily, we have no idea if or when he sleeps or how he gets writing done! (We suspect it has to do with having evil clones.) Stuart is a Chicago native and runs the author resource Horror Tree.*

# There's Always Hope
by Nerisha Kemraj

Fighting a losing battle with the darkness of my own doing, I took my kids out for a final breakfast—it had to be the best.

I paid the bill, ready for the inevitable, when she appeared...

"The world doesn't know what we do for our children...but those who matter, do. So, we do it anyway, and they love us for it. Unconditionally," she said as if she knew the atrocity about to happen.

I was speechless. Her words renewed my hope, my will.

Looking at my grown-up babies now, I smile, knowing that angels live among us.

*Multi-genre (short-fiction) author, and poet, **Nerisha Kemraj**, resides in South Africa with her husband and two, mischievous daughters. She has work traditionally published/accepted in 30 publications, thus far, both print and online. She holds a BA in Communication Science from UNISA and is currently busy with a Post-Graduate Certificate in Education.*
*Facebook: Nerishakemrajwriter*

# Salvation Awaits
## by K.T. Tate

"Welcome to heaven," greets the angel.

I laugh. "But…I'm a serial killer."

"There's no sin here, only God's love. Here, embrace it," they reply, reaching for me.

Unconditional love cascades through my soul, burning away all impurities. The urge to kill evaporates, leaving behind only myself.

*Oh God, what have I done! If I'm not a predator, what am I? Am I a person, also human? The same as those I butchered?* My mind shatters under the weight of realisation.

Panic drops me to my knees. My life plays before me, raw and horrific.

This is hell.

The angel smiles.

*K.T. Tate lives in Cambridgeshire in the UK. She writes mainly weird fiction, cosmic horror and strange monster stories.*
*Website: eldritchhollow.wordpress.com*
*Tumblr: eldritch-hollow.tumblr.com*

# Perpetual Fall
## by Beth W. Patterson

They say that he who humbles himself shall be exalted. It's a really vague and passive statement. And nobody ever spouted wisdom on what to do when the exalted keep falling from grace.

I wonder if the Almighty above was ever so frustrated with angels. It must take divine patience to cope with seraphs constantly plunging headlong from their lofty stations. But I am no deity.

My forebears and my scions are shocked at my outburst. But I'll say it once more in case you didn't hear me: "Look here, you little bitch! Stay on top of our Christmas tree!"

*Beth W. Patterson was a full-time musician for over two decades before diving into the world of writing, a process she describes as "fleeing the circus to join the zoo". She is the author of the books Mongrels and Misfits, and The Wild Harmonic, and a contributing writer to twenty anthologies. Patterson has performed in eighteen countries, expanding her perspective as she goes. Her playing appears on over a hundred and sixty albums, soundtracks, videos, commercials, and voice-overs (including seven solo albums of her own). She lives in New Orleans, Louisiana with her husband Josh Paxton, jazz pianist extraordinaire.*
*Website: www.bethpattersonmusic.com*
*Facebook: bethodist*

# Disputed Possession
## by Shawn M. Klimek

"I give up!" yelled the voice from behind the shed. Two six-shooters sailed into the dirt in quick succession—thump, thump—raising little clouds of dust, and then Molly Paine lurched into the sunlight as though shoved, her hair a black tumbleweed and her dress clinging by a single sleeve. Recovering her balance, she ran into the sheriff's arms.

"He wanted to possess me," she cried, trembling.

"Here, Molly. I've got you," he said, before shouting "Now, come out with your hands up, Nick!"

Too late, the sheriff noticed the malevolent black pits of Molly's eyes.

"Already here," said Nick.

*Shawn M. Klimek is a writer whose other recent anthologies include: "Full Metal Horror 2", by Zombie Pirate Publishing, "Organic Ink" by Dragon Soul Press, "Grumpy Old Gods (Vols. 1 & 2)" by Stormdance Publications, and soon, "Blaze: Inner Circle Writer's Group Flash Fiction Anthology 2019."*
*Website: jotinthedark.blogspot.com*
*Facebook: shawnmklimekauthor*

# Ritual
## by Rickey Rivers Jr.

"Gaze into the chalice."

She did.

"What do you see?"

"I see myself."

"Yes. You are of pure mind and heart."

The surrounding ones nodded.

"Now, grasp the chalice."

She did.

"Drink the red."

The surrounding ones chanted. "Drink the red. Raise the dead."

She peered into the chalice, seeing herself wavy in the liquid. Vignettes of life were shown to her. It made her uneasy.

She stood.

The hooded ones closed in.

"Drink the red," said the main.

As if entranced, she raised the chalice to her lips and let the red coat her tongue.

The dead soon rose.

*Rickey Rivers Jr.* was born and raised in Alabama. He is a writer and cancer survivor. He likes a lot of stuff. You don't care about the details. He has been previously published in Fabula Argentea, ARTPOST magazine, the anthology Chronos, Enchanted Conversations Magazine, (among other publications).
Twitter: @storiesyoumight

# Apocalypse Denied
## by Jonathan Inbody

A hundred thousand angels descended from the clouds with flaming swords, flanked on both sides by heavenly chimera. At the front of the attacking army, the Four Horseman spread destruction with every hoofbeat, pouring wrath and ruin down through the atmosphere and onto mankind's cities below like holy napalm. In the centre of the army rode Yahweh on a golden chariot, glowing brighter than the sun and burning still hotter. His Son rode beside Him, brandishing a whip of thorns. The trumpets sounded, cracking the sky as the end of the world finally arrived.

Humanity returned fire with anti-air missiles.

*Jonathan Inbody is a filmmaker, author, and podcaster from Buffalo, New York. He enjoys B-movies, pen and paper RPGs, and New Wave Science Fiction novels. His short story "Dying Feels Like Slowly Sinking" is due to be published in the anthology Deteriorate from Whimsically Dark Publishing. Jon can be heard every other week on his improvisational movie pitch podcast X Meets Y.*
*Website: xmeetsy.libsyn.com*

# Fallen
## by Jack Wolfe Frost

Darkness. Why had I fallen so far? One hundred years ago I was fighting for truth and light. Or so I thought. I'd always had that rebellious streak. I know why I am fallen, curiosity, but it still sucks. Digging too deep into the master plan and finding that the so-called truth and light had a twisted end plan. And for finding that, I was banished to the dark, a cast down angel.

Light. I look around and see him, I can feel his power. He beckons me, a fire in his eyes.

"Welcome to the Rebellion, Michael," said Lucifer.

*Jack Wolfe Frost is the Eternal Rebel; he rebels against everything which may have the word "rules" or "behave" within it. Born in Sheffield, UK, in 1956; he first started writing in 1982, as a hobby - Now older and wiser, he has had several poems and short stories published.*
*Website: jackjfrost.wordpress.com*
*Twitter: @JackWolfeWriter*

# Shadows
## by Rennie St. James

We await her decision; free will is unique to humans. Even after a millennium, I still wonder how they make their decisions. Humans vacillate between light and dark with the slippery ease of shadows. Her brow is furrowed, her bottom lip sucked between her teeth. A classic human 'thinking' pose.

Still, we wait. Such control lies with these young, ignorant creatures who refuse to be mere pawns.

Do they even understand the power of choosing one's fate? I peer into the darkness seducing many from good. The dark angel grins and winks at me as the human makes her choice.

*Rennie St. James shares several similarities with her fictional characters (heroes and villains alike) including a love of chocolate, horror movies, martial arts, history, yoga, and travel. She doesn't have a pet mountain lion but is proudly owned by three rescue kitties. They live in relative harmony in beautiful southwestern Virginia (United States). The first three books of Rennie's urban fantasy series, The Rahki Chronicles, are available now. A new series and several standalone stories are already in the works as future releases.*
*Website: writerRSJ.com*

# Almost Perfection
## by J.W. Garrett

Her wings fluffed silently, her head bent low, the Kingdom's expectations read.

An angel? *Her*?

She raised her face to the luminosity above, praying for endurance to perform only one "good" deed. She sped toward Earth enjoying the sensations of flight. The night air washed over her, the sight below a shattered magnificence. Appearing before him she smiled, golden halo askew, tilted during her adventure. He stumbled. She closed her eyes. A force flowed through her, sucking out his breath. He gagged, sputtered, fell. Dead. Had he recognised his prey? A horn beckoned her. Her senses perked.

Heaven? Or Hell?

*J.W. Garrett has been writing in one form or another since she was a teenager. She currently lives in Florida with her family but loves the mountains of Virginia where she was born. Her writings include YA fantasy as well as short stories. Since completing Remeon's Quest-Earth Year 1930, the prequel in her YA fantasy series, Realms of Chaos, she has been hard at work on the next in the series, scheduled to release June 2020. When she's not hanging out with her characters, her favourite activities are reading, running and spending time with family.*
*Website: www.jwgarrett.com*
*BHC Press: www.bhcpress.com/Author_JW_Garrett.html*

# No Light, No Angels
## by Stacey Jaine McIntosh

I didn't believe in angels, but then you were taken too soon. Years earlier than any of us ever imagined you would be. And I found myself wanting to believe. I needed to believe in something beyond an earthly, godless existence. But the surrounding air felt still. There was nothing but silence. There would be no comfort for those of us left behind if I couldn't feel anything. How could I find solace if you weren't looking down watching over us? I couldn't. And though I suppressed the pain, I couldn't suppress one thought.

Angels aren't real. They don't exist.

*Stacey Jaine McIntosh was born in Perth, Western Australia where she still resides with her husband and their four children. Although her first love has always been writing, she once toyed with being a Cartographer. Since 2011 she has had over two dozen short stories and drabbles published both online and in various anthologies. She has also had two poems accepted for publication. Stacey is also the author of Solstice, Morrighan & Lost and she is currently working on several other projects simultaneously. When not with her family or writing she enjoys reading, photography, genealogy, history, Arthurian myths and witchcraft. Website: www.staceyjainemcintosh.com*

# The Big Question
## by Dawn DeBraal

Gabriella, Angel of Death, stood on the road, unnoticed by the paramedics.

She'd been sent to this accident to take a good man who had a family. The bad man responsible for the crash drove erratically under the influence, hitting the good man head-on. Gabriella wondered why the bad man was to remain here while the good man died. It was *the big question*. Regardless, today one of them would die.

She sensed another presence standing near. Recognising her indecision, they'd sent another angel to help settle her doubtful mind.

Bending low, Azreal whispered, "I will wrestle you for him."

*Dawn DeBraal lives in rural Wisconsin with her husband, two rat terriers, and a cat. She successfully raised two children (meaning they didn't return to the nest!) After many years serving the government at the Federal and County level, she recently retired. Having extra time on her hands she started to write after a paralyzed vocal cord took her ability to speak for two months. Not finding her voice, she discovered that her love of telling a good story could be written. Her works have been published in Palm-Sized Press, Spillwords, Mercurial Stories, Potato Soup Journal, and Blood Song Books.*

# Interference
## by Jodi Jensen

"Don't do it, Camuel. It's forbidden to interfere."

"There's a baby on the other side of that wall." Standing between the fire and the gas line, Cam glared at the Reaper. "I don't care if you take someone else. But this'll kill the infant, too, and I won't allow that."

"It's not your decision. The fire has been lit. It's time."

Cam extinguished the flames with a simple nod at the faulty dryer. "You cannot have him."

"You'll answer for this."

"I'm sure—"

Camuel was struck down, one of the fallen now.

In exile, he watched the boy grow.

*Jodi Jensen grew up moving from California, to Massachusetts, and a few other places in between, before finally settling in Utah at the ripe old age of nine. The nomadic life fed her sense of adventure as a child and the wanderlust continues to this day. With a passion for old cemeteries, historical buildings and sweeping sagas of days gone by, it was only natural she'd dream of time traveling to all the places that sparked her imagination.*

# Challenging the Gods
### by Kevin Hopson

Tagas watched as Layla stood over the lifeless man. As a messenger for the gods, Tagas could sense Layla's conflict. Despite her divine powers, Layla was still mortal. Her human empathy sometimes clouded her decisions.

"The drought is destroying this town," Layla said. "People are killing one another to survive. Zihnos, God of Rain, could end it all."

"He could," Tagas replied, "but the choice is not yours to make. Your mission doesn't involve saving this town."

"Then I suppose this one life will have to suffice."

She kneeled and rested a hand on the man's chest. His eyelids flickered.

*Prior to hitting the fiction scene in 2009, **Kevin Hopson** was a freelance writer for several years, covering everything from finance to sports. His debut work, World of Ash, was released by MuseItUp Publishing in the fall of 2010. Since then, Kevin has released over a dozen books through MuseItUp, and he has also been published in various magazines and anthology books. Kevin's writing covers many genres, including dark fiction and horror, science fiction and fantasy, and crime fiction.*
*Website: www.kmhopson.com*

# Two Mistakes
## by Rennie St. James

Humans are the ones who differentiate between light and dark. They spin tales fearing the moon while glorying in the sun as if such trivial distinctions matter. Some of the most heinous acts are committed during the bright light of day. Evil thrives in the light and blossoms with an audience.

That is the second mistake made by humans. They believe the support of others justifies their choices. Alone, they might have heard the whisper of their better angels.

Today, it is easier than ever to bring them together during the day, and I always smile as I do so.

*Rennie St. James shares several similarities with her fictional characters (heroes and villains alike) including a love of chocolate, horror movies, martial arts, history, yoga, and travel. She doesn't have a pet mountain lion but is proudly owned by three rescue kitties. They live in relative harmony in beautiful southwestern Virginia (United States). The first three books of Rennie's urban fantasy series, The Rahki Chronicles, are available now. A new series and several standalone stories are already in the works as future releases.*
*Website: writerRSJ.com*

# A Hint of Death
## by Nerisha Kemraj

"Mommy, are angels real?"

Little Eva, squinted as sunlight streamed through the window. Her mom glanced at her through the rear view mirror.

"Some people think so, Sweety." She took the main road towards Eva's daycare.

"Because there's a lady with wings touching your shoulders, Mom. There's a beautiful light around her."

"Aw, that's beautiful, honey." Eva's mom laughed.

"But there's a man with black wings next to me, Mom. He looks scary," Eva whispered.

"That's enough daydreaming for this morning, Eva. Save some for school, okay?" She smiled.

The impact from the truck slammed their car against the barrier.

*Multi-genre (short-fiction) author, and poet, **Nerisha Kemraj**, resides in South Africa with her husband and two, mischievous daughters. She has work traditionally published/accepted in 30 publications, thus far, both print and online. She holds a BA in Communication Science from UNISA and is currently busy with a Post-Graduate Certificate in Education.*
*Facebook: Nerishakemrajwriter*

# Sounds so Easy
## by Austin P. Sheehan

When I recognised the song playing in that god-awful bar I smiled. That bass, those guitars, that voice. Had to be Bowie. As I downed my pint, some of the punters sang along, raucously shouting the chorus—'*WE CAN BE HEROES!*' The voices of that sinful choir echoing around the dingy dive—chock-full of city scum—gave me a sense of sublime irony.

I laughed, placing the empty glass on the wooden bar, and ordered another. "He makes it sound so damn easy!" I grinned a vile and bloody grin as the bartender shook her head and pulled my beer.

*Austin P. Sheehan is a writer of speculative fiction, a lover of language, literature and '90s TV. Armed with a psychology degree, he went into the world to study humanity, and now prefers the company of his wife and their greyhounds. He grew up in the valleys of Victoria's high country, and despite living in Melbourne, always feels at home amongst the mountains. You'll often find mountains in his stories, whether they're sci-fi, fantasy or alternative history.*
*Website: austinpsheehan.com*
*Twitter: @AustinPSheehan*

# The New Recruit
## by William J. Joel

"I don't know how to use this," she said, giggling. I adjusted the flaming sword in her hands.

"Here," I said, "less tightly on the grip, so you won't feel the strike in your hands."

She smiled, brushing back locks of golden, angelic hair. Then she kissed me, on the lips. I pulled back as quickly as I could.

"Stop that!" I yelled. "Stop that behaviour this moment, recruit!"

She laughed. "You're cute when you're angry."

I turned around so she wouldn't see the blood rushing to my cheeks.

I never saw her red claws before they pierced my throat.

*All things are connected. That's the premise of what **William J. Joel** does. Each of Mr. Joel's interests informs each other. Mr. Joel has been teaching computer science since 1983 and has been a poet even longer. His poems have appeared in Chronogram, Common Ground Review, and Gravel Magazine.*
*Website: www.aniprof.com*

# Where Even a God Must Die
## by Terry Miller

Jayson traded wings for horns but was permitted to keep them; a gift from Lucifer himself. The horns grew at once, upward, downward, and curling repeatedly to their fine point. They were more magnificent than he had imagined.

Jayson stepped out, with newfound confidence, onto the skull-stoned streets of the Underworld where succubi danced with all manner of abominable vermin. He fancied himself a god amongst such loathsome creatures. The succubi soon took notice, seductively they moved toward him. Jealous vermin, dripping with saliva, pounced him. What manner of place is this, he thought, where even a god must die?

*Terry Miller is an author and 2017 Rhysling Award-nominated poet residing in Portsmouth, OH, USA. He has self-published a dark poetry collection on Amazon and one short story to date. His work has also appeared in Sanitarium, Devolution Z, Jitter Press, Poetry Quarterly, O Unholy Night in Deathlehem, and the 2017 Rhysling Anthology from the Science Fiction and Fantasy Poetry Association.*
*Facebook: tmiller2015*

# One Last Chance
## by Matthew M. Montelione

A dishevelled man with twitching eyes was about to enter a store when he was stopped by a handsome man.

"Wait!" the gentleman yelled, "you're going to rob the attendant at gunpoint, correct?"

The thief paused.

"I made him fall asleep. I'll wake him up, unless you give me what's left of your morality."

"Err…sure."

The gentleman smiled. "Go in."

The thief entered.

A figure in white appeared next to the gentleman.

"You had one last chance, Reginald," she said.

"Better to be evil than boring," Reginald said as he scratched his back, the remnants of his tattered wings.

*Matthew M. Montelione is a horror writer born and raised on Long Island in New York. His stories have been published in Quoth the Raven: A Contemporary Reimagining of the Works of Edgar Allan Poe, Thuggish Itch: Devilish, and other titles. Matthew is also an American Revolution historian who focuses on the local experiences of Loyalists on Long Island. His work on the subject has been published in Long Island History Journal and Journal of the American Revolution.*
*Website: maybeevils.com*
*Twitter: @maybeevils*

# Knocking on Heaven's Door
## by Shelly Jarvis

"Beer?"

Zaqiel shakes her head, disgusted.

"Suit yourself," I say, popping the cap from a Natty Light. I take a swig as I look her over. She's ragged, worn down, a contrast to the warrior I normally see. I can tell she doesn't want to be here, but she's got no other choice. I cut to the chase and ask, "What's wrong?"

She flinches. "There's a problem. In Heaven."

I try to stop my smile, but I can't. "Yeah?"

"An attack. We need your help."

"You want a demon's help?"

"All the demons."

Her words sober me. "Who attacked?"

"Humans."

*Shelly Jarvis is a speculative fiction author from West Virginia, US. She found a life-long love of sci-fi and fantasy in the 3rd grade when she found Madeleine L'Engle's "A Wrinkle in Time." Shelly is an avid reader, a Whovian, the ideal viewer of dog rescue videos, and undoubtedly Ravenclaw. She currently has two YA sci-fi books available for purchase on Amazon.*
*Website: www.ShellyJarvis.com*

# Oblivious
## by Carole de Monclin

The teenager didn't pay attention to the man she'd just passed on the crowded street, but he noticed her. I saw the way he looked back at her. When he turned around and started following her, my errands became irrelevant.

I trailed the man who trailed the girl.

On the subway platform, as he was slipping inside a train behind her, I jostled him. The doors closed before he recovered, and the train left without him. I apologised and walked away.

The girl was safe.

Guardian angels come into our lives unseen. Today, it'd been my turn to be one.

*Carole de Monclin has lived in France and Australia, but for the moment the USA is home. She finds inspiration from her travels. She loves Science Fiction because it explores the human mind in a way no other genre can. Plus, who doesn't love spaceships and lasers? Her stories appear in the Exoplanet Magazine and Angels - A Dark Drabbles Anthology.*
*Website: CaroledeMonclin.com*
*Twitter: @CaroledeMonclin*

# Gary's Visitor
## by Gabriella Balcom

"Gary, if the pain gets unbearable, just push the button." The nurse then left.

He grimaced at the morphine drip.

"Dad, you don't have to endure pain," his son Vince commented. Gary's body had been ravaged by an incurable, particularly-nasty and fast-spreading cancer. "Taking painkillers makes sense."

"They knock me out, and I don't want to sleep through my remaining time."

Later a sound woke him. A different nurse stood nearby. She seemed to glow.

"You're a good man," she said, taking his hand.

Warmth moved throughout his body. His pain vanished.

The next day, testing showed he was cancer-free.

*Gabriella Balcom lives in Texas with her family, loves reading and writing, and thinks she was born with a book in her hands. She works in a mental health field, and writes fantasy, horror/thriller, romance, children's stories, and sci-fi. She likes travelling, music, good shows, photography, history, interesting tales, and animals. Gabriella says she's a sucker for a great story and loves forests, mountains, and back roads which might lead who knows where. She has a weakness for lasagne, garlic bread, tacos, cheese, and chocolate, but not necessarily in that order.*
*Facebook: GabriellaBalcom.lonestarauthor*

# Late Night Seminar
## by Derek Dunn

Cliff passed the conference room on his way to the custodial closet. The religious fanatics were still in there. Dozens had gathered for the spiritual seminar.

He'd heard bits and pieces as he roamed the halls, waiting to lock up for the night.

"The angels will deliver us."

"Truth will be restored."

It wasn't anything new. But this time, he stopped. The speaker, a beautiful young woman, had dropped her clothes and stood naked on the stage.

Maybe this was the religion for him, Cliff thought. But then, her skin peeled away as horns protruded from a scaly flesh beneath.

*Derek Dunn lives in the American Northwest with his family. He's a film enthusiast and musician who writes primarily horror and mystery stories.*
*Twitter: @DerekTDunn*

# The Fall
## by Zoey Xolton

Lucifer stared into the Abyss, brow furrowed in thought. Had he made the right decision? *Yes*, he was certain of it. His legion of Fallen Angels awaited his command. A third of the Heavenly Host had fought alongside him for the right to free-will; something God's pathetic humans were gifted and had not the good nature to be grateful for.

Looking over his shoulder at his loyal brothers and sisters, he raised his bloodied fist. The signal. Into the void between Heaven and Earth they dove, black wings spread.

*Better to rule in Hell*, thought Lucifer, *than serve in Heaven.*

*Zoey Xolton is an Australian Speculative Fiction writer, primarily of Dark Fantasy, Paranormal Romance and Horror. She is also a proud mother of two and is married to her soul mate. Outside of her family, writing is her greatest passion. She is especially fond of short fiction and is working on releasing her own themed collections in future.*
*Website: www.zoeyxolton.com*

# A Surprising Truth
## by Stuart Conover

It might surprise humans that the eternal struggle between Heaven and Hell wasn't that great of a deal to those involved.

Azmuth, Devourer of Souls, was currently sitting across the table discussing world politics with Devi, the Bringer of Light, while enjoying an iced coffee in the largest chain in the world.

Both sides took credit for its success.

"I really don't know how you drink these without cream and sugar," Azmuth murmured, stirring his drink.

"And I don't know how you don't drink it black," Devi replied.

This would be the greatest disagreement the two would have all day.

*Stuart Conover is a father, husband, rescue dog owner, published author, blogger, journalist, horror enthusiast, comic book geek, science fiction junkie, and IT professional. With all of that to cram in daily, we have no idea if or when he sleeps or how he gets writing done! (We suspect it has to do with having evil clones.) Stuart is a Chicago native and runs the author resource Horror Tree.*

# Designated Driver
## by Gregg Cunningham

"One more, Tony, then we're going. Okay?"

"Sure. Whatever you say, Trevor."

Tony knocked back his sixth lager and raised his hand for the barman.

"Two lagers and a coke for the poof." He winked, pointing back at Trevor who was now checking his watch.

"I mean it Tony; I'm going in five!"

The girl Tony was impressing was even more pissed than he was.

"Fuck it. You're on your own, mate."

***

The cop pulled Trevor over.

"Blow into the mouthpiece, please."

"When was your last drink, sir?"

Tony you bastard!

The breathalyser bleeped as Trevor began to worry.

*Gregg Cunningham 48, short story writer who has had to pick up his game since stumbling into facebook writer's groups. He has stories published by 559 Publishing in in 13 Bites volume 3,4,5, Plan 9 from Outer space, Other Realms, Heard It on The Radio, 559 Ways to Die, short stories publishing by Zombie Pirate Publishing in Relationship add Vice, Full Metal Horror, Phuket Tattoo, World War four and Flash Fiction Addiction (flash) with Zombie Pirate Publishing, and also in Daastan Magazine Chapter 11 and Brian,Rich and the Wardrobe.*
*Amazon: www.amazon.com/-/e/B016OTHX0K*

# Ambition
## by Joel R. Hunt

Asriel paced back and forth, wringing his hands. He had thought being a guardian angel would be easy. That's what the others had told him.

*If your human has impure thoughts, give them visions of Hell. That always scares them back on track.*

Well, it hadn't worked.

He'd caught his human having very dark thoughts indeed, so Asriel had appeared with dire warnings, conjuring sights and sounds of Hell's burning pits and everlasting torture. Asriel had expected his charge to scream and cry, plea for mercy and pray for redemption.

Instead, the human had grinned, eyes lit up with hunger.

*Joel R. Hunt is a writer from the UK who dabbles in the darker aspects of life, particularly through horror, science fiction and the supernatural. He has been published here and there (though likely nowhere you've heard of) and hopes to have released his first anthology of short stories later this year.*
*Twitter: @JoelRHunt1*
*Reddit: JRHEvilInc*

# No Vacancy
## by John H. Dromey

Harry and Maud Greenwald's holiday did not go well. Maud's mother-in-law, suffering from dementia, went with them. They couldn't find a pet sitter so Fluffy went, too.

In a small café, the elder Mrs Greenwald was listless and only picked at her food.

Later, something remarkable happened as they passed an ancient burial site.

"Harry!" Maud said. "The vacant look just went out of your mother's eyes."

The next morning Maud called her sister. "I have good news and bad. Harry's mum got her appetite back— we don't know what malevolent demon possessed her, but she ate the family dog."

**First published in *Daily Bites of Flesh 2011: 365 Days of Horrifying Flash Fiction* by Pill Hill Press, 2010**

*__John H. Dromey__ was born in northeast Missouri, USA. He enjoys reading—mysteries in particular—and writing in a variety of genres. He's had short fiction published in Alfred Hitchcock's Mystery Magazine, Martian Magazine, Stupefying Stories Showcase, Thriller Magazine, Unfit Magazine, and elsewhere, as well as in a number of anthologies, including Chilling Horror Short Stories (Flame Tree Publishing, 2015).*

# Why I Chose to Fall – A Memoir
## by Carole de Monclin

Life widowed me twice, but Heaven reunited us all.

I worried it'd be awkward. I still passionately loved both my husbands.

But after crossing the Pearly Gates, I became ethereal and lost any need or desire for food, enjoyment, and sex.

What's the use of being young forever if you spend eternity lounging on a cloud, serenely bored?

We discreetly contacted Satan and negotiated terms. No torture or scorching flames for us. Satan was willing to help to spite his father.

And we fell.

Is Hell perfect? No, but I'll take fun and excitement over perfection any day of eternity.

*Carole de Monclin* has lived in France and Australia, but for the moment the USA is home. She finds inspiration from her travels. She loves Science Fiction because it explores the human mind in a way no other genre can. Plus, who doesn't love spaceships and lasers? Her stories appear in the *Exoplanet Magazine* and *Angels - A Dark Drabbles Anthology*.
Website: CaroledeMonclin.com
Twitter: @CaroledeMonclin

# Spirit Guide
## by J.D. Bell

The drug runners left Joe Running Bear in the desert to die; payment for interference with their operation on the reservation.

Wandering in the blazing heat a vision came to him, a being adorned in red and yellow feathers. "I am a Kashina, your spirit guide," the vision said. "Be strong. I will show you the path home."

The spirit guided Joe home to safety. "You have one more task to complete before your journey is finished," the spirit told him. Days later, Joe informed on the gang. They were killed in a fierce gun battle with the local authorities.

*J.D. Bell is an award-winning, internationally published, author of flash fiction and short stories. He recently retired from the world of writing advertising copy and is now enjoying the universe of creative fiction.*
*Facebook: jim.writes.stories*
*Twitter: @JimBell58*

# Keeping Score
by William J. Joel

It lowered its feet into the lava, letting molten stone slowly heal its wounds. Another sat next to it.

"We lost," the second said. The first lifted its head.

"I know."

"Is that all you're gonna say?"

The first leaned back against its stone seat. "What do you want me to say?"

The second shook its head. "We lost. Humanity is now on God's side. All that work, and for what?"

The first one smiled. "We only lost a battle."

"A battle?"

The first laughed. "Yep, a battle. Universe is huge, and Earth's only one experiment."

"Oh," replied the second.

*All things are connected. That's the premise of what **William J. Joel** does. Each of Mr. Joel's interests informs each other. Mr. Joel has been teaching computer science since 1983 and has been a poet even longer. His poems have appeared in Chronogram, Common Ground Review, and Gravel Magazine.*
*Website: www.aniprof.com*

# Angel in the Dark
## by Ximena Escobar

The memory of her wings was as heavy as the fallen men she'd let down, all the souls she wanted to save but couldn't. She'd been cast from heaven because she'd been seen; because she craved humanity and got too close.

Will anyone see her now?

Her eyes bore the bluest of a sky of day, but her lack of experience made it impossible for humans to connect with her. They were drawn to her beauty—they adored her like poetry, like the divine—but she needed a weight heavier than wings. The weight of flesh. And she needed angels.

*Ximena Escobar is an emerging author of literary fiction and poetry. Originally from Chile, she is the author of a translation into Spanish of the Broadway Musical "The Wizard of Oz", and of an original adaptation of the same, "Navidad en Oz". Clarendon House Publications published her first short story in the UK, "The Persistence of Memory", and Literally Stories her first online publication with "The Green Light". She has since had several acceptances from other publishers and is working very hard exploring new exciting avenues in her writing.*
*She lives in Nottingham with her family.*
*Facebook: Ximenautora*

# You Pick the Nicest Places
by Stephen Herczeg

Michael nursed his drink. His white suit, shirt and tie and black leather shoes shone in the dark bar.

Ashtaroth, in midnight black, sat nearby. He laughed at the other patrons.

They wore denim jeans and black leather jackets with a winged skull on the back.

Ash said way too loud, "Losers. They're not Hell's Angels, they're a bunch of pansies."

A bikie approached them.

"Outside now, we're sick of your crap."

Ash rose, "This should be the most fun since the great battle for heaven."

Michael shook his head, "You pick the nicest places."

He followed the demon outside.

*Stephen Herczeg is an IT Geek based in Canberra Australia. He has been writing for over twenty years and has completed a couple of dodgy novels, sixteen feature length screenplays and numerous short stories and scripts. His horror work has featured in Sproutlings, Hells Bells, Below the Stairs, Trickster's Treats #1 and #2, Shades of Santa, Behind the Mask, Beyond the Infinite; The Body Horror Book, Anemone Enemy, Petrified Punks and Beginnings. He has also had numerous Sherlock Holmes stories published through the Belanger Books - Sherlock Holmes anthologies.*

# An Old Priest
## by David Bowmore

Sweat ran down the old man's temples as he entered the room.

The old woman, in her bed, looked at him with hate filled eyes. She was one of his most devout congregates and he barely recognised her. Steam, along with the scent of hell, rose from her body.

When he'd been younger, exorcism had been a problem only specialist priests dealt with. This was his fifth in a month. Though his faith was strong, his body was weak. Could he keep this up?

He readied the holy water and the crucifix.

"Begone, Satan, inventor and master of all deceit!"

*David Bowmore has lived here, there and everywhere, but now lives in Yorkshire with his wonderful wife and a small white poodle. He has worn many hats in his time; head chef, teacher and landscape gardener. His first collection of short stories 'The Magic of Deben Market' is available from Clarendon House.*
*Website: davidbowmore.co.uk*
*Facebook: davidbowmoreauthor*

# Last Rites
## by William J. Joel

"Pray for me."

"What?"

"I asked you to pray for me."

"That's what I thought I heard. No, I will not pray for you."

"Why not?"

"Because."

"Because?"

"Because…you're a demon."

"And?"

"Seriously? You want an angel to pray for a demon?"

"But I'm dying."

"I know. So am I. Battle's over."

"And no one won."

"I know."

"We're all going to die, soon."

"I know."

"So…please…pray for me."

"Okay. I'll pray for you. To whom should I pray."

"Does it truly matter?"

"Of course it matters!"

"Really? In death there are no sides."

*All things are connected. That's the premise of what **William J. Joel** does. Each of Mr. Joel's interests informs each other. Mr. Joel has been teaching computer science since 1983 and has been a poet even longer. His poems have appeared in Chronogram, Common Ground Review, and Gravel Magazine.*
*Website: www.aniprof.com*

# Prisoner
## by Cecelia Hopkins-Drewer

Kiki bent to smell the flower. It was a rare experience for a black angel, imprisoned, locked away because her side had lost the latest round in the never-ending battle between good and evil. The only problem was that no one knew which side was good any longer.

Her jailor appeared in the greenhouse doorway, a tall, bright angel of white. "Are you ready?" she asked.

"Five minutes more," Kiki begged. "What does it matter, when we have eternity?"

"Rules are rules," Ophy replied. "Time's up!"

Kiki gave the flower a hungry look and then returned obediently to her cell.

*Cecelia Hopkins-Drewer is a speculative fiction writer, poet and scholar, who lives in Adelaide, South Australia. She has also written a Masters paper on H.P. Lovecraft, and a teenage vampire series that commences with "Mystic Evermore". Her science fiction poetry has been published in "The Mentor" a fanzine edited by Ron Clarke.*
*Amazon: amazon.com/Cecelia-Hopkins-Drewer/e/B071G968NM*

# Origin
## by Stephen Oram

I can't see very well, but I know that when the signal is given it will be a speedy resolution.

The call is given: "Ascend." And thousands upon thousands of us move as one to the tiny speck sometimes known as angel dust. Our aim? To answer, once and for all, how many of us can fit on a pinhead.

We could become permeable, merging our heavenly bodies, but it's banned. It's a shame, really. Instead, we push and pull, our wings get torn and without thinking, I bite the angel next to me and my inner evil is born.

*Stephen Oram writes science fiction and is lead curator for near-future fiction at Virtual Futures. He enjoys working collaboratively with scientists and future-tech people - they do the science he does the fiction. He is published in several anthologies and has two published novels, Quantum Confessions and Fluence. His collection of sci-fi shorts, Eating Robots and Other Stories, was described by the Morning Star as one of the top radical works of fiction in 2017 and his second collection Biohacked & Begging was published in April 2019.*
*Website: www.stephenoram.net*
*Twitter: @OramStephen*

# After the Bombings
by Michael Kellichner

"So, you're here, too?"

The demon looked at the angel smoking a cigarette atop a hill of shattered concrete exuding twisted, rusted metal. "Don't like my handiwork?"

"*Your* handiwork?"

"Of course. Angry hearts of men and such."

The angel scoffed. "This is punishment for wickedness."

"Just like you to try and take credit for this."

"Was thinking the same thing."

Wind whistled through hollow eyes where windows used to be. "Got any more of those?"

The angel tossed down a crumpled pack, then a chrome lighter. The demon pulled out a cigarette, lit it, nodded his approval at their work.

*Michael Kellichner is a writer and poet from Pennsylvania currently living in South Korea. Other short fiction of his has been published in Black Denim Lit, Trigger Warnings: Short Fiction with Pictures, and Three Crows Magazine.
Twitter: @mithalanis*

# Secret Plan
## by Kelly A. Harmon

"Bumper crop of priests today," the imp said, shackling the priest.

"Earthquake in Rome—" Father Michalski grunted from pain, "as foretold."

The imp consulted his clipboard. "Don't they teach you 'the road to Hell is paved with good intentions'?"

Father Michalski shrugged.

Around Hell, priests caught each other's eyes and nodded. "By the power of God, we expel you!" they chanted over and over, under their breath, then louder.

The prayer was joined by the all the clergy who had gone before.

*Boom!*

All the demons were cast from Hell.

Shackles fell from the priests' wrists.

And God owned Hell.

*Kelly A. Harmon is an award-winning journalist and author, and a member of the Science Fiction & Fantasy Writers of America and Horror Writers of America. A Baltimore native, she writes the Charm City Darkness series. The fourth book in the series, In the Eye of the Beholder, is now available. Find her short fiction in many magazines and anthologies, including Occult Detective Quarterly; Terra! Tara! Terror! and Deep Cuts: Mayhem, Menace and Misery. Website: kellyaharmon.com*
*Twitter: @kellyaharmon*

# An Angel Enchanted
## by Terry Miller

Michael. No, not that one. He was no archangel, rather he's quite low in the hierarchy. Nevertheless, his wings were strong, his sword sharp.

The year was 1692. Michael was deemed to walk the earth and keep watch, incognito, over the Father's creation. He obeyed.

There was a stench about Salem, the air was rife with it. Michael's journey led him to its door, but he made it no further before Mary's gaze summoned his own. That night, they knew one another. The morning found a village pillaged, beheaded; but for a select few. This is history lost to legend.

*Terry Miller is an author and 2017 Rhysling Award-nominated poet residing in Portsmouth, OH, USA. He has self-published a dark poetry collection on Amazon and one short story to date. His work has also appeared in Sanitarium, Devolution Z, Jitter Press, Poetry Quarterly, O Unholy Night in Deathlehem, and the 2017 Rhysling Anthology from the Science Fiction and Fantasy Poetry Association.*
*Facebook: tmiller2015*

# A Reason to Hang On
by Shawn M. Klimek

The condemned murderer stood on the gallows platform, his back stooped like a wilted flower, waiting his turn to be hanged. On either side stood his executioner and a priest. To his rear, two invisible angels.

"You likely won't be needed," said the dark angel.

"Sometimes they repent at the last instant as I nudge their conscience," said his white-winged counterpart. "Timing is everything."

"You make me ashamed of my pessimism," said the dark angel. "Here, I'll help by reminding him of his wife."

"But he murdered his wife," said the light angel.

"Oops, my bad," said the dark angel.

*Shawn M. Klimek is a writer whose other recent anthologies include: "Full Metal Horror 2", by Zombie Pirate Publishing, "Organic Ink" by Dragon Soul Press, "Grumpy Old Gods (Vols. 1 & 2)" by Stormdance Publications, and soon, "Blaze: Inner Circle Writer's Group Flash Fiction Anthology 2019."*
*Website: jotinthedark.blogspot.com*
*Facebook: shawnmklimekauthor*

# The Seraph and the Demon
by Pamela Jeffs

The seraph and the demon face each other, eyes locked. A cradle rocks gently between them, the tiny form of a sleeping girl-child within. "The babe belongs with us," says the seraph calmly.

"The child belongs to Hell," replies the demon.

"But she is innocent!"

"Her parents were not."

"And so, Lucifer claims the child to pay for the sins of the parents?"

"Yes—when those sins outweigh the good in the child."

The seraph frowns. "But she is the last of God's children."

The demon shrugs, "God should have been watching. Should have prevented his humans from destroying Earth."

*Pamela Jeffs* is a speculative fiction author living in Queensland, Australia with her husband and two daughters. She is a member of the Queensland Writers' Centre and has had numerous short fiction pieces published in recent national and international anthologies. In 2017 and again in 2018, Pamela was nominated for an Australian Aurealis Award in the category of 'Best Science Fiction Short Story'. Her debut collection titled 'Red Hour and Other Strange Tales' was released in March 2018.
Website: www.pamelajeffs.com
Facebook: pamelajeffsauthor

# Proper Demonic Etiquette
## by Carole de Monclin

Nana always said he was the sweetest demon, always willing to do her bidding. Messing up the odds at Bingo, spilling drinks on her granddaughter's rivals' dresses, whispering to my dad's boss a raise was due.

He made life easier.

But Nana is gone, and I need help. I want Troy to notice me.

Long ago, she explained how to summon her demon: pentacle, chicken blood, and candles.

"Who dares?" Nana's demon thunders.

"I'm Violet's granddaughter."

"I knew her. But you, human, have not been properly presented to me. Rule breakers deserve no mercy."

He smiles wickedly before he pounces.

*Carole de Monclin* has lived in France and Australia, but for the moment the USA is home. She finds inspiration from her travels. She loves Science Fiction because it explores the human mind in a way no other genre can. Plus, who doesn't love spaceships and lasers? Her stories appear in the *Exoplanet Magazine* and *Angels - A Dark Drabbles Anthology*.
Website: CaroledeMonclin.com
Twitter: @CaroledeMonclin

# The Devil Made Me Do It
## by Gregg Cunningham

Do you know how many times I have heard that tired, lame excuse?

It makes me laugh every time one of you lot kneel before me weeping, begging for mercy or pleading for redemption.

If it were up to me, I'd send you all back down to that hoofed demon to talk to him about the contract fine print.

But, no. I'm meant to be the all forgiving Saint Peter; here to greet all you sinners at the pearly gates with a loving smile.

Well, here's a revelation…

The Devil didn't make you do it.

*He* did.

*He* was bored.

*Gregg Cunningham 48, short story writer who has had to pick up his game since stumbling into facebook writer's groups. He has stories published by 559 Publishing in in 13 Bites volume 3,4,5, Plan 9 from Outer space, Other Realms, Heard It on The Radio, 559 Ways to Die, short stories publishing by Zombie Pirate Publishing in Relationship add Vice, Full Metal Horror, Phuket Tattoo, World War four and Flash Fiction Addiction (flash) with Zombie Pirate Publishing, and also in Daastan Magazine Chapter 11 and Brian,Rich and the Wardrobe.*
*Amazon: www.amazon.com/-/e/B016OTHX0K*

# Sanctify
## by Adam S. Furman

Have you observed Her? She stumbles and falls. She's beautiful. You can see a piece I left in Her heart where the Light shines. But darkness surrounds it. She cannot do this by Herself. She causes Her own pain, trapped as the creature She has been borne into. Her actions are rubbish compared to the Light I left.

But watch for my guidance. Her cries? I will cast into a song. Her mourning? I will transform into a dance. Her pain? I will mould into joy.

By my hand, I shall purify Her. By my actions, I shall sanctify Her.

*Adam S. Furman* *lives in rural Illinois with his family which includes a lot of kids (like...a lot). He generally writes science fiction.*
*Twitter: @AdamSFurman*

# School's Out
## by Beth W. Patterson

My first school was ablaze.

The flames shot from floor to ceiling sparing nothing in the nursery: smiling, colourful jungle animals painted on the walls, baby swings, toys, and records. An angel carried me down the fiery corridor to the classroom that had been for the pre-schoolers, and I watched the short tables and chairs scorch and melt into the floor. The place where I had first learned to speak French and read basic books was now engulfed in the same firestorm.

"Why doesn't the fire hurt me?" I asked.

The angel sadly replied, "Your innocence had already been destroyed."

*Beth W. Patterson was a full-time musician for over two decades before diving into the world of writing, a process she describes as "fleeing the circus to join the zoo". She is the author of the books Mongrels and Misfits, and The Wild Harmonic, and a contributing writer to twenty anthologies. Patterson has performed in eighteen countries, expanding her perspective as she goes. Her playing appears on over a hundred and sixty albums, soundtracks, videos, commercials, and voice-overs (including seven solo albums of her own). She lives in New Orleans, Louisiana with her husband Josh Paxton, jazz pianist extraordinaire.*
*Website: www.bethpattersonmusic.com*
*Facebook: bethodist*

# Angelic Selfie
## by Nerisha Kemraj

Her wings touched the ground before she did.

"Do we have to save him? He wants to die."

"Yes, we do. It's not his time."

"Why though? It's what he wants. Doesn't Father always give them what they want?"

"No, He gives them what they need."

"Psht, whatever. What a waste of time. I could be taking selfies instead. Hey, let's take one now!" She posed, her face next to his.

"Come now, child. You have a lot to learn," Hyperion said, brushing the gadget away.

Delilah rolled her eyes.

*Child!* As if he was any older than her.

*Multi-genre (short-fiction) author, and poet, **Nerisha Kemraj**, resides in South Africa with her husband and two, mischievous daughters. She has work traditionally published/accepted in 30 publications, thus far, both print and online. She holds a BA in Communication Science from UNISA and is currently busy with a Post-Graduate Certificate in Education.*
*Facebook: Nerishakemrajwriter*

# Killing Makes Me Happy
## by C.H. Williams

As I hold the knife above his heart, the devil on my shoulder hisses, "Do it."

The angel tells me, "Don't!"

They're really there, the devil and angel; actually, physically present, sat on my goddamn shoulders. Where did you think the stories started? From ancient paintings, borne of the minds of ancient painters? No.

I have a tiny angel on one shoulder, always saying dumb stuff like, 'Don't kill people," and, "Put the knife down."

And the tiny devil, my pal, my buddy, actually gives really great advice like, "Sure, you should kill them," and, "Do what makes you happy."

*C.H. Williams is a full-time mum who writes adult contemporary fiction, short stories, flash pieces and poetry. She can often be found with a jar of peanut butter in one hand and a bar of dark chocolate in the other, which coincidentally makes it rather difficult to type.*
*Twitter: @authorch*
*Instagram: @c.h.writes*

# The Tall Guy
## by Stephen Herczeg

I'm done. Everything's blurry. Breathing's hard. It won't be long now.

Stupid. I stood up to check the enemy. A sniper got me. Good shot. Straight in the chest. Threw me back against the trench wall.

Just wait until the tall guy gets here.

I'm happy. I'll see Mum, Dad, my brother. All gone.

The darkness comes.

Then a blinding light. A beautiful man stands before me, with wings spread wide.

"But I thought…"

He smiles.

"Taller? Wearing black? Skeletal face?"

I nod.

"You humans made him up."

He reaches down.

"Come, take my hand. We have far to go."

*Stephen Herczeg is an IT Geek based in Canberra Australia. He has been writing for over twenty years and has completed a couple of dodgy novels, sixteen feature length screenplays and numerous short stories and scripts. His horror work has featured in Sproutlings, Hells Bells, Below the Stairs, Trickster's Treats #1 and #2, Shades of Santa, Behind the Mask, Beyond the Infinite; The Body Horror Book, Anemone Enemy, Petrified Punks and Beginnings. He has also had numerous Sherlock Holmes stories published through the Belanger Books - Sherlock Holmes anthologies.*

# A Hell of a Good Idea
## by R.G. Halstead

Garrett really had to laugh. The nerve of some people. The *audacity*!

"Wow. What a bold and daring phone scam. That jerk with the thick accent trying to sell me visits from Heavenly angels. Nice fecking try. I can just imagine what that scumbag scammer looks like. Probably a real, *actual* demon from the depths of Hell."

Taking another drink from his eighth beer today, he continued, "A demon with a pretty damn good idea. I think I'll try the same scam; but have more success than that...that demon. I can be a Hell of a lot more persuasive."

*R.G. Halstead, a 63-year-old, takes to writing late in his life. Influences? Those old Alfred Hitchcock Mystery Magazines from the late 1950s and the 1960s with the great twisty endings. Love them.*

# Jetpack
## by Phil Dyer

It's not a jetpack. The first wings don't emerge at your shoulders, not for anyone, and you can't fly with your first. Ankles and knees are common, occasionally wrists. The Holy Spirit seeks egress in mysterious ways. Continue hunting demons.

After your fifth kill, your wings will begin to feel stronger. You will have many, now. There will be more. You may feel lighter, buoyed with purpose. This is a miracle. The Spirit hollows your bones to feed more feathers.

Eat forty demons. Allow the Spirit to emerge, engorged and fluttering. Spread the sporing glory of your wings and fly.

*Phil Dyer does medical research in Liverpool and writes spec fic on the side. His stories have appeared in Unfit Magazine, 101 Words and The Drabble. He retweets animal videos.*
*Twitter: @ez_ozel*

# Even Cats Get Halos
by Alanna Robertson-Webb

I miss my guardian angel.

I used to call him Furball, since I was never good at naming pets, but he didn't seem to mind.

He looked like your typical black cat, and he saved my life when he was just a kitten; I was planning on shooting myself the night I stumbled upon him, and I couldn't bring myself to ignore an injured kitten who had been thrown into a dumpster to die.

Furball's gone now, but I know he's still watching over me. I bet he has wings, and a fish-shaped halo.

I'll never forget my best friend.

*Alanna Robertson-Webb is a sales support member by day, and a writer and editor by night. She loves VT, and live in PA. She has been writing since she was five years old, and writing well since she was seventeen years old. She lives with a fiance and a cat, both of whom take up most of her bed space. She loves to L.A.R.P., and one day she aspired to write a horrifyingly fantastic novel. Her short horror stories have been published before, but she still enjoys remaining mysterious.*
*Reddit: MythologyLovesHorror*

# Girdle
## by Umair Mirxa

Gaelan steadied his sword and tightened his grip on the hilt. He sensed his own fear in those around him. They were the last line of defence for the City of Light, and there were too few of them.

The girdle of enchantment protecting the city broke, and ten thousand demons flooded in. Now all that stood between them and absolute victory were the Keepers of the Wall.

Gaelan watched as, one by one, his fellow angels fell. He followed suit and dropped to his knees. When the Keepers rose again, it was as champions in the demon army's vanguard.

*Umair Mirxa lives in Karachi, Pakistan. His first published story, 'Awareness', appeared on Spillwords Press. He has also had stories accepted for anthologies from Zombie Pirate Publishing, Blood Song Books, Fantasia Divinity Magazine and Publishing, and Iron Faerie Publishing. He is a massive J.R.R. Tolkien fan, and loves everything to do with fantasy and mythology. He enjoys football, history, music, movies, TV shows, and comic books, and wishes with all his heart that dragons were real.*
*Website: www.umairmirxa.com*
*Facebook: UMirxa12*

# Lucifer
## by Stacey Jaine McIntosh

Of all the angels in existence, it had to be Lucifer.

He was once God's favourite, but since the fall, God didn't seem to be listening to him much anymore. He, along with his brothers, had sought comfort in the arms of willing young women, but despite the short-lived pleasure, Lucifer was restless.

Perhaps that was because Lilith called to him.

The bible depicted her as a creature of the night, devourer of children, but it hadn't always been so. In fact, if it hadn't been for him and Leviathan, perhaps Lilith would have remained the girl she once was.

*Stacey Jaine McIntosh was born in Perth, Western Australia where she still resides with her husband and their four children. Although her first love has always been writing, she once toyed with being a Cartographer. Since 2011 she has had over two dozen short stories and drabbles published both online and in various anthologies. She has also had two poems accepted for publication. Stacey is also the author of Solstice, Morrighan & Lost and she is currently working on several other projects simultaneously. When not with her family or writing she enjoys reading, photography, genealogy, history, Arthurian myths and witchcraft. Website: www.staceyjainemcintosh.com*

# Angel of Mercy
## by Brian Rosenberger

Crucified on a wooden pillar configured from shipping pallets. Nails driven through wrists and ankles. Nude. A body Playboy approved.

An angel without wings. Confusing. Her halo burns away all doubt.

How she got here, no one knows nor cares.

Some of us, most of us, went elsewhere to pray.

Then, she entered our lives.

We renounced all Gods. Now we worship her. Only her.

When She bleeds, we all bleed.

Some worshippers call her the Angel of Mercy.

Maybe.

To me, she is the Angel of No Mercy.

I grip my baseball bat.

Disappoint an angel, you invite Hell.

*Brian Rosenberger lives in a cellar in Marietta, GA (USA) and writes by the light of captured fireflies. He is the author of As the Worms Turns and three poetry collections. He is also a featured contributor to the Pro-Wrestling literary collection, Three-Way Dance, available from Gimmick Press.*
*Facebook: HeWhoSuffers*

# Loss
## by Simon Clarke

With the night forever long, I cleave to home anchored by sorrow.

Then I hear an angel sing and feel the sweet breeze of dark wings beating grey, exhausted air. But nothing changes. An evil miasma sucks at my legs, amorphous shapes forming into sensuous arms and offering another solution. But nothing changes.

Despite all my knowledge and practice, all my rituals, all the sacrifices, both bloody and sweet, I cannot escape this feeling. Oh, I'll think it out and I'll know, I always know; not now though, not yet until they have my soul. Then I will be free.

*Simon Clarke was born in and raised and currently resides in East Anglia, United Kingdom. He has been writing fiction for at least five years and regularly submits to UK and international publications as well as reading short pieces and poetry at open mic events. He is currently working on his first novel and continues to write short stories and poetry.*

# Pillows
## by Lynne Lumsden Green

Contrary to the rumours, Lucifer's pillows aren't stuffed with feathers discarded from his own wings. Where's the fun in that? Nor are they stuffed with baby birds, as they would squirm and peep.

Those pillows are trophies. Every time he defeats one of God's angels, they must forfeit a feather. Every time another soul is lost to heaven, those pillows get plumper and softer.

Whenever someone does a good deed, one of the feathers evaporates. If you want Lucifer to sit on ashes and coals, be kind to all of humankind and animals. Give evil a kick in the buttocks.

*Lynne Lumsden Green has twin bachelor's degrees in both Science and the Arts, giving her the balance between rationality and creativity. She spent fifteen years as the Science Queen for HarperCollins Voyager Online and has written science articles for other online magazines. Currently, she captains the Writing Race for the Australian Writers Marketplace on Facebook. She has had speculative fiction flash fiction and short stories published in anthologies and websites.*
*Website: cogpunksteamscribe.wordpress.com*

# Troubles
## by Matthew M. Montelione

Peter, my guardian angel, put his hand on my shoulder. "You must trust yourself. Repeatedly fretting about trivial matters will rip your mind apart. You'll stray from your center, which took you long to find," he said with a kind smile. That smile always comforted me in times of trouble. But these days, troubles were a constant friend. The weight of my suspect thoughts burdened me everyday.

I caught a shadow out of the corner of my eye. Colt, my dark angel, had arrived.

Peter sighed. "I will never give up on you, my child."

I walked over to Colt.

*Matthew M. Montelione is a horror writer born and raised on Long Island in New York. His stories have been published in Quoth the Raven: A Contemporary Reimagining of the Works of Edgar Allan Poe, Thuggish Itch: Devilish, and other titles. Matthew is also an American Revolution historian who focuses on the local experiences of Loyalists on Long Island. His work on the subject has been published in Long Island History Journal and Journal of the American Revolution.*
*Website: maybeevils.com*
*Twitter: @maybeevils*

# Fallen Feathers
## by Brandy Bonifas

The truck swerved, barely missing the child running into the road. Nobody saw Nathanael shielding the boy, or the invisible scattering of feathers. A mother, sobbing grateful tears, gathered the child in her arms.

Nathanael's mentor appeared. "You are an angel of death."

"But they're only children."

"You can't save them all." He indicated the feathers blowing away on the breeze. "Once they're gone, you will fall."

Nathanael felt his next call. A burning building, a trapped girl. He shielded her until firefighters arrived. Nobody noticed the charred feathers smouldering in the flames.

Nathanael fell.

He awoke, scarred…and mortal.

*Brandy Bonifas lives in Ohio with her husband and son. Her work has appeared or is forthcoming in anthologies by Clarendon House Publications, Pixie Forest Publishing, Zombie Pirate Publishing, and Blood Song Books, as well as the online publications CafeLit and Spillwords Press.*
*Website: www.brandybonifas.com*
*Facebook: brandybonifasauthor*

# Touched by an Angel
## by J. Farrington

It was the trial of the century; it was meant to awaken the world's spirituality. Instead, the world descended, divided; those who welcomed the angel's arrival, and those who preached his sinister motives.

He came from the heavens and swept up the abandoned child, took her in his arms and rose above them all, embracing the child. A feeling of dread filled those who watched. An eye witness account swears his actions were less than holy.

The eye witness, an elderly man, gave the damning evidence.

The jury condemned the angel. Execution, the sentence.

The devil was in the detail.

*J. Farrington* *is an aspiring author from the West Midlands, UK. His genre of choice is horror; whether that be psychological, suspense, supernatural or straight up weird, he'll give it a shot! He has loved writing from a young age but has only publicly been spreading his darker thoughts and sinister imagination via social platforms since 2018. If you would like to view his previous work, or merely lurk in the shadows...watching, you can keep up to date with future projects by spirit board or alternatively, the following;*
*Twitter: @SurvivorTrench*
*Reddit: TrenchChronicles*

# The Battle of Purgatory
## by Matthew M. Montelione

"Hold the doors!" Raphael yelled as he braced himself for the final battle between his archangels and the demons. His tunic was soaked with blood.

Gabriel was weary. "Commander, is not Purgatory a middle ground between our forces and those of Hell? Many have been lost in this war."

Raphael's eyes blazed like white-hot fire. "Do you not see, brother? Winning Purgatory grants us the majority. We must claim it! Now! For the Kingdom!"

War trumpets blasted.

The doors burst asunder. Satan's soldiers charged in, waving the banners of Hell.

Raphael and his archangels crashed upon them like roaring thunder.

*Matthew M. Montelione is a horror writer born and raised on Long Island in New York. His stories have been published in Quoth the Raven: A Contemporary Reimagining of the Works of Edgar Allan Poe, Thuggish Itch: Devilish, and other titles. Matthew is also an American Revolution historian who focuses on the local experiences of Loyalists on Long Island. His work on the subject has been published in Long Island History Journal and Journal of the American Revolution.*
*Website: maybeevils.com*
*Twitter: @maybeevils*

# Young Lion
## by David Bowmore

This is what most beings don't understand; there is no good or evil.

Only right or wrong.

Some people kill. Doesn't mean they're evil. Happens all the time in the wild.

Chimpanzees will turn on each other. A young lion will defeat an old patriarch to claim the pride.

That is what I intend to do; take His crown and throne. He has made a mess of everything; Earth has never been in such turmoil, and the less said about Heaven, the better.

I've right on my side.

*I am the archangel Gabriel, and I will be your new God.*

*David Bowmore has lived here, there and everywhere, but now lives in Yorkshire with his wonderful wife and a small white poodle. He has worn many hats in his time; head chef, teacher and landscape gardener. His first collection of short stories 'The Magic of Deben Market' is available from Clarendon House.*
*Website: davidbowmore.co.uk*
*Facebook: davidbowmoreauthor*

# A Praying Man Preyed Upon
by Rickey Rivers Jr.

The colour and location of the room shifted.

"I understand! You are tempted when holy."

"You believe yourself holy?"

He gave no answer. His eyes darted as he prayed.

The women who were not women surrounded him, tasting him. Their tongues like lit matches.

"Please, stop!"

"But you don't want that, not really."

They continued, advancing to biting toes, fingers and nipples.

"Stop it! Why is this happening to me?"

"You don't know? Remember where you go to get your jollies?"

His breathing stuttered. His own tongue fought against him.

They covered him, pulling and stretching. He screamed until segmentation.

*Rickey Rivers Jr. was born and raised in Alabama. He is a writer and cancer survivor. He likes a lot of stuff. You don't care about the details. He has been previously published in Fabula Argentea, ARTPOST magazine, the anthology Chronos, Enchanted Conversations Magazine, (among other publications).*
*Twitter: @storiesyoumight*

# An Alternate Armageddon
## by Aiki Flinthart

"They are destructive fools, these humans." I sat on a crag of granite and overlooked the vast, crawling city. Grey-brown haze blurred the blue sky to ash.

"*He* loves them, Gusion," Adriel replied. "What do you see?"

I snarled, gesturing with a claw. "Besides this mewling tide of pestilence?" I peered into the future and grimaced. "I see no Armageddon between us, brother."

Adriel's pale brows rose. "But it is foreordained. Our final battle will lay waste to the Earth. Humanity will be judged."

Rising, I turned away. "The Earth is already laid to waste. They have judged themselves unworthy."

*Aiki Flinthart has had short stories shortlisted in the Aurealis awards and top-8 listed in the USA Writers of the Future competition, as well as published in various anthologies and e-mags. She has 11 published spec fic novels and has edited 2 short story anthologies. She regularly gives workshops on writing fight scenes at conventions. Lives in Brisbane. Does martial arts, archery, knife throwing and lute-playing.*
*Website: www.aikiflinthart.com*

# Fresh Meat
## by Gregg Cunningham

"You stabbed me you bastard!" The man stared at the butcher's knife stuck in his chest as he stumbled back from the cash register.

"Sure did," the cashier said nonchalantly, pointing up at the security camera.

"Cameras are off as well. It's just your word against mine mate," He smiled, opened the cash register, and picked up his phone.

"But…But, I only came in for a couple of rump steaks!" The man gurgled, falling to the bloody floor.

"Yeh, sorry. Business is slow. No point in having insurance if you ain't gonna use it, eh!"

"Hello…police? I've been robbed!"

*Gregg Cunningham 48, short story writer who has had to pick up his game since stumbling into facebook writer's groups. He has stories published by 559 Publishing in in 13 Bites volume 3,4,5, Plan 9 from Outer space, Other Realms, Heard It on The Radio, 559 Ways to Die, short stories publishing by Zombie Pirate Publishing in Relationship add Vice, Full Metal Horror, Phuket Tattoo, World War four and Flash Fiction Addiction (flash) with Zombie Pirate Publishing, and also in Daastan Magazine Chapter 11 and Brian,Rich and the Wardrobe.*
*Amazon: www.amazon.com/-/e/B016OTHX0K*

# Stolen Words
## by Harsh Ramchandani

I wasn't even supposed to be home till after school, which explains why the letter beside him was addressed to my mother.

He was expecting her to find him. He was expecting her to read that letter, scribbled with his words of hate and bitter resentment.

I couldn't let her see that.

I felt as sick reading it as I was writing its replacement. Tears rolled off my cheeks and onto the page which was now filled with lies expressing his sorrow. I left it beside him, beside his motionless body. For her to find it and find her peace.

*Harsh Ramchandani is from Hong Kong. A graduate in Media Arts from the University of Plymouth, he has always been interested in creating content and has recently found great joy in writing. While he mostly writes poetry, he occasionally ventures into the world of flash fiction. Website: harshchan.com*

# Singe Me
## by Jo Seysener

Wisps of smoke twirled upward wherever he touched her wings. The cave reeked—brimstone and halos never mixed well. That holy glow—he sneered, running a claw down the pristine beast's soft skin. It parted like butter, emitting a bright light. The heart of an angel's presence.

The wound healed swiftly. His tongue swept out, tasting the moans of his prey. Almost too easy. But the only way to do lasting damage was to burn away the feathers protecting the bone structure of their wings.

Devoid of their soft downy feathers, an angel looked just like a demon.

*Jo Seysener is a mum of three crazies, a scatter of chickens, a decrepit kelpie and a rambunctious GSD. She lives with her husband near Brisbane, Australia. When she is not exposing her kids to cult story books from her childhood, she can be found in the kitchen experimenting with new flavours and pairings. She adores alpacas.*
*Facebook: joseysener*
*Website: www.joseysener.com*

# Gabriel
## by Stephen Herczeg

The couple turned down a dark alley.

"It's a shortcut."

"It's scary."

A shadowy figure stepped into the dim light, a gun levelled at them.

"Everything. Now."

He grabbed Marta's pearls, snapping them free to rain across the filthy ground.

From behind, "Stop."

A figure ran between the couple and their assailant.

The gun fired.

Light blazed as a flaming sword met the bullet.

"Begone from here and reconsider your choices," a voice boomed.

The mugger ran.

Tom spoke to the dazzling figure, "Who are you?"

The apparition turned, his wings spread wide, "I'm Gabriel, I'm here to help."

*Stephen Herczeg is an IT Geek based in Canberra Australia. He has been writing for over twenty years and has completed a couple of dodgy novels, sixteen feature length screenplays and numerous short stories and scripts. His horror work has featured in Sproutlings, Hells Bells, Below the Stairs, Trickster's Treats #1 and #2, Shades of Santa, Behind the Mask, Beyond the Infinite; The Body Horror Book, Anemone Enemy, Petrified Punks and Beginnings. He has also had numerous Sherlock Holmes stories published through the Belanger Books - Sherlock Holmes anthologies.*

# Birth of Evil
## by Melissa Neubert

Labour had been going on for hours and she was exhausted. Salty sweat dripped off her face and with each contraction she felt like she was being ripped apart, which she was. With one last push her baby entered the world. She heard his first cry.

The nurses dried him off and handed him to her. She looked down at her son hoping for a miracle. She didn't get it. He had red eyes and horns, just like his father, the Devil. Evil found her nine months ago. He had seduced her and impregnated her. Her son was a monster.

*Melissa Neubert was born in the Pacific Northwest and currently lives in Illinois with her husband, three children and two dogs. Melissa has been a daycare provider, veterinary assistant, teacher/library aide, and administrative assistant. Melissa travels extensively both domestically and internationally where she finds inspiration for her writing in beautiful and unique locations. When she is not writing she enjoys music, reading, concert and wildlife photography, football and camping. Although Melissa has been writing since grade school, she has only recently begun pursuing the craft seriously. She writes mostly in the genres of Suspense/Thriller and Adult Paranormal Romance.*

# Fealty
## by Umair Mirxa

Faelynn threw back her hood and let her wings unfold. Dark as the pit they spread from her back, casting a vast shadow over the motley assembly before her.

"Kneel, and swear eternal fealty," she thundered. "Pledge your miserable existence and rise as champions of Death."

They fell to their knees, thousands as one. Murderers, rapists, and adulterers—sinners, all of them.

A shadow greater than her own loomed, and Faelynn smiled at the hand on her shoulder.

"You have done well, child," said the first of the Fallen. "The muster is complete. Let the invasion of Heaven begin."

*Umair Mirxa lives in Karachi, Pakistan. His first published story, 'Awareness', appeared on Spillwords Press. He has also had stories accepted for anthologies from Zombie Pirate Publishing, Blood Song Books, Fantasia Divinity Magazine and Publishing, and Iron Faerie Publishing. He is a massive J.R.R. Tolkien fan, and loves everything to do with fantasy and mythology. He enjoys football, history, music, movies, TV shows, and comic books, and wishes with all his heart that dragons were real.*
*Website: www.umairmirxa.com*
*Facebook: UMirxa12*

# Tipping Point
## by Lynne Lumsden Green

You live your life from tip to tip. At birth, you are tipped from the bottle of your mother's womb in a flood of amniotic fluid. When you die, your ashes are tipped into an urn or dirt is tipped upon your coffin in the grave. Your entire life is just a tipping point.

At birth, there is a guardian angel set to watch over you. The angel weighs your soul, setting your good deeds against your evil ones. If you cross the tipping point, expect a warm welcome when you die…the angel will be guarding against you.

*Lynne Lumsden Green has twin bachelor's degrees in both Science and the Arts, giving her the balance between rationality and creativity. She spent fifteen years as the Science Queen for HarperCollins Voyager Online and has written science articles for other online magazines. Currently, she captains the Writing Race for the Australian Writers Marketplace on Facebook. She has had speculative fiction flash fiction and short stories published in anthologies and websites.*
*Website: cogpunksteamscribe.wordpress.com*

# Storm
by Anika Claire

One wrathful angel descends, and another rises to meet it, warm from basking in the sun near its earthly charges. High above soft, vaporous white surfaces, ethereal beings glare at one another. Each taunts the other for the first move, wings wide, scowls dark. Then all is a blur as they leap forward to meet.

Bright sparks fly as swords clash, wild winds whipped up by frantic wing-beats as they duck and weave, driving one way then another in a manic dance.

Silvery, iridescent droplets of blood fall in rain, and later, shining tears fall gently on the restless ocean.

*Anika Claire* lives in Brisbane, Australia with her young family, where she alternates between making maps and escaping to other worlds, through either reading or creating them. You can find her reviewing and podcasting about books at;
Website: teainthetreetops.com
Instagram: @anni.treetops

# Revelation
## by Alanah Andrews

The angels appeared as silent statues standing sentry around the world. One in every town, and three or four in each major city. They arrived under the cloak of darkness, so when the morning sun dawned, the bloody smear of sunrise glinted off their wings.

Proud and still, they watched us—unmoving—for days.

Confusion reigned. Were they here to protect us, or was there something more sinister at play?

21st December, seven days after the angels first arrived, they finally delivered their message. Speaking in unison, the familiar phrase shattered our souls.

"The hour of His judgment has come."

*Alanah Andrews writes speculative fiction and spends far too much time debating whether 1984 or The Handmaid's Tale are most representative of our future. Her YA dystopian novel about a future where emotions are forbidden, Eve of Eridu, was released in 2018. She has also had several short stories published in a range of different places. When she's not writing, Alanah runs the Australian Speculative Fiction group, teaches high school English, and attempts to raise two children. She has a husky, a pony, a blue-tongue lizard, and dreams of travelling Australia in a bus.*
*Website: www.alanahandrews.com*
*Facebook: alanahandrewsauthor*

# A New Beginning
## by Ximena Escobar

Threads of her hair drop like a rainbow curtain as she opens her heavy eyelids; heavy with red and pain unfelt as she lies on the hardest soothing sunshine; tiny crystals like sugar shining but she can't feel their sharpness, just the delightful heat like a hug; like lying on the edge of the pool as a child, quenching a thirst for warmth and gravity.

Suddenly, she rises. Not she, another. She will never be *her*, spread in the distant concrete like a crooked mannequin.

She ascends, pulled by another's wings; those of the new she that she will be.

*Ximena Escobar is an emerging author of literary fiction and poetry. Originally from Chile, she is the author of a translation into Spanish of the Broadway Musical "The Wizard of Oz", and of an original adaptation of the same, "Navidad en Oz". Clarendon House Publications published her first short story in the UK, "The Persistence of Memory", and Literally Stories her first online publication with "The Green Light". She has since had several acceptances from other publishers and is working very hard exploring new exciting avenues in her writing.*
*She lives in Nottingham with her family.*
*Facebook: Ximenautora*

# Heaven/Hell Bingo
## by Sinister Sweetheart

The ball's retrieved and read aloud.

"N9."

Damabiath stamped a wave design on his card. "All nine members of the Naval crew will survive the typhoon."

Another ball rolls into place.

"I17."

Akatash stamped her card. "Seventeen killed in tonight's ice storm," she proudly reported.

"G48."

Dearg-Due smashed a bloody thumbprint on her card. "Forty-eight people around the World get Gonorrhea today!" The room groaned. "Everything's so inappropriate with you Dearg!" Aynaet snarked with daggered eyes.

"B74."

Akriel's booming laugh resonated; fists raised high in triumph. "BINGO! Seventy-four babies born across the world on this day; completely healthy and loved!"

*Since **Sinister Sweetheart** made her first post to a popular Internet forum, she's taken the horror community by storm. Her ability to create, terrify, and drive home her stories is insurmountable. Sinister Sweetheart's published works can be found in multiple anthologies for all to read, but be forewarned, if you do... you may want to call your therapist after, her stories are terrifying, disturbing and devilishly unsettling. She is not only a fright visually, but also has a creepy tentacle in horror podcasting as well. Sinister Sweetheart writes, voice acts and is the media director of the Scarecrow Tales podcast.*
*Website: Sinistersweetheart.wixsite.com/sinistersweetheart*
*Facebook: NMBrownStories*

# The Trumpet
## by Will Shadbolt

On a particularly hot July afternoon the angels appeared. They looked like thin, beautiful humans, with osprey-brown, canoe-sized wings sprouting from their backs. One holding a trumpet, later identified as Gabriel, proclaimed God was dead, and blew his instrument.

Nothing happened. No lightning. No earthquakes. No storms.

What it signalled was worse.

"Struck Him down myself," Gabriel said. "The old bastard kept us all as slaves..."

Their faces began to melt into horns and scabs. Their wings shed their feathers; they were as scaly as a dragon.

"And you'll soon see what He put us through," the demon Gabriel said.

*Will Shadbolt has lived across the world, including in Germany and China. He currently works in NYC. His fiction has appeared in Daily Science Fiction and numerous drabble anthologies.*

# In the Silence
## by Raven Corinn Carluk

The Seventh Seal opened. Heaven fell silent.

Into that silence came a threnody. From the mountains, mankind's cries and pleas rose as a song of their pain and plight.

A hymn begging for mercy.

Michael looked upon an Earth ravaged by the previous Seals. An Earth the Almighty had created and commanded the angelic hosts to love. An Earth that could have been guided back to a Heavenly path.

This was not righteous or just. This was malicious torture.

Michael turned to the throne, flaming sword gripped tight in his hand. The Second Rebellion started not from pride, but pity.

*Raven Corinn Carluk is an indie author of dark fantasy and paranormal romance.*
*Website: RavenCorinnCarluk.Blogspot.Com*

# Out of Eden
## by Zoey Xolton

Raziel watched events unfold from atop the walls of Eden. Already, Adam's first wife, Lilith, had been cast out of Eden for questioning her inferior place as a woman. She believed she was equal to a man. God thought otherwise.

Now Eve, the second wife, had partaken of the fruit of the Tree of Knowledge; Adam following suit. God was a fickle, domineering and jealous Father. *Perhaps Lucifer had been right?* No matter. As the mortals exited Eden, Raziel flew down, gifting them the Sepher Raziel, the Book of Secrets. Hopefully, it would help them survive what was to come…

*Zoey Xolton is an Australian Speculative Fiction writer, primarily of Dark Fantasy, Paranormal Romance and Horror. She is also a proud mother of two and is married to her soul mate. Outside of her family, writing is her greatest passion. She is especially fond of short fiction and is working on releasing her own themed collections in future.*
*Website: www.zoeyxolton.com*

# Feathers for the Children
by Terry Miller

The world is full of sorrow. For this, the angels weep. The sky clouds, the ducts of the heavens, pour down their sympathetic tears. The oceans fill, the rivers swell, and the creeks spill from their banks while the Fallen One and his angels stoke the embers of Hell's flames; the reservoirs of sympathy lift from the earth as a result of the infernal furnace's heat.

This is the cycle, eternal, with man caught in the middle, unaware. Swords clash, feathers scattered to the winds of changing seasons. A dove? A raven? Black and white keepsakes for a child's collection.

*Terry Miller is an author and 2017 Rhysling Award-nominated poet residing in Portsmouth, OH, USA. He has self-published a dark poetry collection on Amazon and one short story to date. His work has also appeared in Sanitarium, Devolution Z, Jitter Press, Poetry Quarterly, O Unholy Night in Deathlehem, and the 2017 Rhysling Anthology from the Science Fiction and Fantasy Poetry Association.*
*Facebook: tmiller2015*

# A Storm in His Hand
by Shelly Jarvis

Guardian angel my ass. The moment he realised we were caught, he bailed. He's no guardian—he's not even a decent friend!

Not that I expected more. Or at least, I shouldn't have. Everybody knows angels do their own thing, in their own time. I was an idiot to think Ramiel was different.

The manacles on my wrists are too tight, cutting into my flesh. I wish I would've stayed home, called in sick, and let the big boys handle it this time.

Distant thunder pulls me from self-pity and a smile tugs my lips. Ramiel rides with the storm.

*Shelly Jarvis is a speculative fiction author from West Virginia, US. She found a life-long love of sci-fi and fantasy in the 3rd grade when she found Madeleine L'Engle's "A Wrinkle in Time." Shelly is an avid reader, a Whovian, the ideal viewer of dog rescue videos, and undoubtedly Ravenclaw. She currently has two YA sci-fi books available for purchase on Amazon.*
*Website: www.ShellyJarvis.com*

# Justice
## by A.S. Charly

The once green grass is covered in blood. Breathing hard, the last two warriors charge at each other, only to both thud to the ground.

Dead and dying soldiers piled up as far as the eye can reach.

Afar, the two kings meet in disappointment. Unable to come to an agreement, they exchange threats in the politest manner, till they call upon the heavens for guidance.

The clouds part, and a golden light blinds everyone. Flags snap, as the whirring of huge wings fills the air. Blindfolded, an angel looks at the kings. With her sword, she beheads them both.

*A.S. Charly loves to lose herself in fantastical worlds far away between the stars, filled with magic and wonder. She also writes and draws when she is not roaming through the park with her children. Her stories have been published in various anthologies and online publications.*
*Facebook: A.S.Charlydreams*

# Angels on the Wall
## by G. Allen Wilbanks

I see angels.

They perch on the walls and stare down at me in my hospital bed. They watch over me with concern and love in their dark eyes. I don't know why. Perhaps my time is drawing near, and they are preparing to take me away from this world of doctors and nurses and medicines that make me feel sick.

The nurse comes in with a syringe. The angels do not like her. When she gives me my shot, they hide from her and I will not see them again for hours. But they will return.

They always do.

**Originally Published in *Drabblz Magazine Issue #3* in August 2018**

*G. Allen Wilbanks is a member of the Horror Writers Association (HWA) and has published over 50 short stories in various magazines and on-line venues. He is the author of two short story collections, and the novel, When Darkness Comes.*
*Website: www.gallenwilbanks.com*
*Blog: DeepDarkThoughts.com*

# God's Pawn
## by Rowanne S. Carberry

Azrael puts his hand to his belt, clutching the hilt of his blade. Tears fill his eyes as he knows what he must do.

Reluctantly he pulls out the sword.

"Ferro igni," he shouts, the blade instantly engulfed by flame.

Only one person in the crowd notices the man surrounded by flame and his eyes fill with fear.

"No, no," he screams at the sky above, "please not now."

Azrael walks forward, a silent prayer to his father to stop this now.

Seconds later his blade plunges through the man's chest. The tears spill as again; he's his father's pawn.

*Rowanne S. Carberry was born in England in 1990, where she stills lives now with her cat Wolverine. Rowanne has always loved writing, and her first poem was published at the age of 15, but her ambition has always been to help people. Rowanne studied at the University of Sunderland where she completed combined honours of Psychology with Drama. Rowanne writes to offer others an escape. Although Rowanne writes in varied genres each story or poem she writes will often have a darkness to it, which helped coin her brand, Poisoned Quill Writing – Wicked words from a poisoned quill.*
*Facebook: PoisonedQuillWriting*
*Instagram: @poisoned_quill_writing*

# I Pray With My Fists
by Morgan Chalfant

Every night, I pray with my fists.

A blood-stamped angel on a white plaster wall. My altar.

It lingers, not listening. No different from any other angel. Just watching. Dirtier—bloodier—than those hovering on high, as am I. Its wings unfold. My anger unravels. With each strike, I bear my sacrament to the indifferent cosmos.

Each blow sends wind to red wings. The mark of every knuckle etches more feathered divinity. I pray alone. I'll finish alone. Some nights this room is my castle, some it's my prison. Maybe, when the bloody angel finally answers me, I'll stop killing.

*Morgan Chalfant is a native of Hill City, Kansas. He received a Bachelor's degree in writing and a Master's degree in literature from Fort Hays State University. His short story, "The Steel Music Box" appeared in the horror anthology, Dark and Evil. Another of his stories, "Little Neon" will be appearing in the forthcoming anthology, Crash Code.*
*Facebook: themorgancchalfant*

# Final Act
## by Hari Navarro

The angel fought for aeons atop the great bluff that juts out above the roof of the universe, her bare feet braced into its crumbling edge.

One day, she tires of the violence and steps backward, arms stretched, the wisp of her feathered back ruffling as she plummets. She dies, or least as close to death as any immortal could ever hope. All she wants is peace.

Down into the void the great sword in her hand cleaves through worlds, and the mass of her body pulverises civilisations as forever she tumbles and falls.

These are the acts of gods.

*Hari Navarro has had work published at the very fine online flash fiction portal 365tomorrows.com, BREACH - a bi-monthly online zine for SF, horror and dark fantasy short fiction and AntipodeanSF - Australia's longest running online speculative fiction magazine. Hari was the Winner of the Australasian Horror Writers' Association [AHWA] Flash Fiction Award 2018 and has, also, succeeded in being a New Zealander who now lives in Northern Italy with no cats.*
*Facebook: HariDarkFiction*
*Twitter: @HariFiction*

# Soul Eaters
## by Eddie D. Moore

Azazel watched from a dark corner of the nursery. Red eyes reflected the moonlight illuminating the room through the pink curtains. A soft growl rumbled deep in his throat as he stepped closer. A malicious smile spread across his face when he looked into the crib.

He spoke in a soft voice. "Once, I was an angel charged with protecting innocent souls, but I found it much more satisfying to consume them, especially if I've taken the time to get to know them."

The baby opened silver eyes and Azazel took a frightened step back. "I thought I knew you!"

*Eddie D. Moore travels extensively for work, and he spends much of that time listening to audio books. The rest of the time is spent dreaming of stories to write and he spends the weekends writing them. His stories have been published by Jouth Webzine, Kzine, Alien Dimensions, Theme of Absence, Devolution Z, and Fantasia Divinity Magazine.*
*Website: eddiedmoore.wordpress.com*

# Early Withdrawal
## by Dawn DeBraal

Bennie had a good angel on his right shoulder, a bad angel on the left. He stood in line at the bank with a note demanding money.

Sweating profusely in his disguise, he fought with both of the angels as he drew closer to the teller. The good angel told him to walk out. The bad angel told him to stick to the plan.

A lady standing near Benny tapped his shoulder. Benny jumped.

"I'm sorry, you dropped this." She handed Benny the stick-up note. Embarrassed, Benny took the note, changing his mind, deciding to let the good angel win.

*Dawn DeBraal lives in rural Wisconsin with her husband, two rat terriers, and a cat. She successfully raised two children (meaning they didn't return to the nest!) After many years serving the government at the Federal and County level, she recently retired. Having extra time on her hands she started to write after a paralyzed vocal cord took her ability to speak for two months. Not finding her voice, she discovered that her love of telling a good story could be written. Her works have been published in Palm-Sized Press, Spillwords, Mercurial Stories, Potato Soup Journal, and Blood Song Books.*

# Keeping Up With the Mending
## by Brandy Bonifas

Haziel, in her rocker, worked on her mending. A little girl played on the floor, unaware.

Boel appeared and Haziel spread her wings.

"I'm here for my charge, not yours," the demon said.

Haziel draped the mended soul around the girl's shoulders.

Boel slipped, instead, inside her father who threw an empty beer can at her. "Look at this mess you've made! You're as worthless as your mother…" He passed out before he could come after her.

Boel slipped back into the shadows. Haziel retrieved the tattered soul from the girl. Assessing the new holes, she returned to her mending.

*Brandy Bonifas lives in Ohio with her husband and son. Her work has appeared or is forthcoming in anthologies by Clarendon House Publications, Pixie Forest Publishing, Zombie Pirate Publishing, and Blood Song Books, as well as the online publications CafeLit and Spillwords Press.*
*Website: www.brandybonifas.com*
*Facebook: brandybonifasauthor*

# The Winning Team
## by Wondra Vanian

Pastor Jim planned his sermon with the enthusiasm of an overworked little league coach. Honestly, he didn't care who won or lost anymore.

If his parishioners thought faith was difficult to sustain, they fell short of how impossible it became when one was the leader, rather than the flock. He carried each of their doubts, fears, and sins.

Disgusted, he shoved the half-written sermon away. He was tired of lying, of pretending.

A voice spoke from behind Pastor Jim. "Maybe it's time to play for the other team..."

Turning slowly, he stared in horror at the towering figure of Lucifer.

*Wondra Vanian is an American living in the United Kingdom with her Welsh husband and their army of fur babies. A writer first, Wondra is also an avid gamer, photographer, cinephile, and blogger. She has music in her blood, sleeps with the lights on, and has been known to dance naked in the moonlight. Wondra was a multiple Top-Ten finisher in the 2017 and 2018 Preditors and Editors Reader's Poll, including ithe Best Author category. Her story, "Halloween Night," was named a Notable Contender for the Bristol Short Story Prize in 2015.*
*Website: www.wondravanian.com*

# False Salvation
## by Crystal L. Kirkham

Long ago, a glorious being commanded, "Bow before this symbol of God and you will find salvation." People listened, believing it to be an angel from on high.

One day, a man came to them and said, "Do not worship as you have. You have been deceived and lead astray. Salvation does not lie in prayers to a symbol, but in the deeds you do."

Few listened to his words, fewer still obeyed and, when he returned to Heaven, he found it empty. He'd given them choice, and they'd chosen blind worship of a symbol over kindness to each other.

***Crystal L. Kirkham** resides in a small hamlet west of Red Deer, Alberta. She's an avid outdoors person, unrepentant coffee addict, part-time foodie, servant to a wonderful feline, and companion to two delightfully hilarious canines. She will neither confirm nor deny the rumours regarding the heart in a jar on her desk and the bottle of reader's tears right next to it. Her paranormal urban fantasy series, Saints and Sinners, is available on Amazon and her YA Fantasy, Feathers and Fae will be released October 11, 2019, from Kyanite Publishing.*
*Website: www.crystallkirkham.com*

# Through the Mirror, Exiled
## by Aiki Flinthart

I stand before the shadowed mirror, my soul in light, my heart in darkness. One finger hovers, inches from the glass. Each day I return, hoping he won't be here. Knowing he will. My imprisoned demon lover. Murderer.

He lies, huddled in Stygian gloom. A bleak stone cell. Through his window, a moonless night. Through mine, a glistening day of brilliance and birdcalls.

His gaunt form rises. Haunted eyes silently pleading. His hands splay on glass.

One touch of my finger would release him back into the light, my world. My heart.

To wreak death again.

I hesitate.

I touch.

*Aiki Flinthart* has had short stories shortlisted in the *Aurealis awards* and top-8 listed in the *USA Writers of the Future* competition, as well as published in various anthologies and e-mags. She has 11 published spec fic novels and has edited 2 short story anthologies. She regularly gives workshops on writing fight scenes at conventions. Lives in Brisbane. Does martial arts, archery, knife throwing and lute-playing.
*Website: www.aikiflinthart.com*

# Blood Red Wings
## by Rowanne S. Carberry

Springing from the ground, black wings spiralling upwards towards an inky sky, he looks down in despair at the devastation.

Blood so dark that unless you knew the smell, could see the glisten and destruction, you may not notice it at first.

Tears spill from his face as a merciless laugh sounds from behind him.

Turning he's blinded.

"Sister, what have you done?" he asks the white-winged evil.

"What you were too weak to do," she sneers at him.

She lands on the ground, dipping her wings in the blood and he's helpless but to watch as they turn red.

*Rowanne S. Carberry was born in England in 1990, where she stills lives now with her cat Wolverine. Rowanne has always loved writing, and her first poem was published at the age of 15, but her ambition has always been to help people. Rowanne studied at the University of Sunderland where she completed combined honours of Psychology with Drama. Rowanne writes to offer others an escape. Although Rowanne writes in varied genres each story or poem she writes will often have a darkness to it, which helped coin her brand, Poisoned Quill Writing – Wicked words from a poisoned quill.*
*Facebook: PoisonedQuillWriting*
*Instagram: @poisoned_quill_writing*

# No Bounds
## by A.R. Johnston

She looked down from the clouds, taking in the beauty below. With a snap, her wings went wide, the feathers iridescent, shimmering in the morning light. She leapt, diving to the lands below, riding the air currents. She landed in a crouch, wings sweeping over her like a cloak before she stood tall.

"Shall we begin anew?" A deep dark voice spoke.

Her smile bright as she turned to see the gorgeous man standing there waiting. Her angel, her demon. He was what made her fall from grace. There could be no other way. Love held and knew no bounds.

*A.R. Johnston is a small-town girl from Nova Scotia, Canada. Her style of writing is considered Urban Fantasy. Her first major publication is part of an anthology called First Love and she has several more titles lined up. She is a lover of coffee, good tv shows, horror flicks, and reader of books. She pretends to be a writer when real life doesn't get in the way. Pesky full-time job and adulting!*

# Enticing
## by A.R. Johnston

He looked up, watching the glorious descent of the angel that was falling from grace. His grin was one that, to some, might have seemed sinister. He knew he was considered a gorgeous man; it was one of the reasons he was a top demon in the legions of Hell. Using it to his advantage to gather souls, entice them to the so-called dark side.

He watched her land, then stand in her glorious form. She was beautiful. His heart beat faster. Was this more than he thought?

"Shall we begin anew?" he asked, placing a kiss beneath her ear.

*A.R. Johnston is a small-town girl from Nova Scotia, Canada. Her style of writing is considered Urban Fantasy. Her first major publication is part of an anthology called First Love and she has several more titles lined up. She is a lover of coffee, good tv shows, horror flicks, and reader of books. She pretends to be a writer when real life doesn't get in the way. Pesky full-time job and adulting!*

# No Going Home
by A.R. Johnston

Black and white. That's all there was left. Black and white feathers strewn every which way. It was the only thing left to show they had ever been here. The white feathers were opalescent in their beauty, the black ones shone like polished obsidian.

Absolute total destruction of one's wings would have been extremely debilitating and painful beyond measure. Yet neither angel nor demon was here to prove that it had been done.

How could either of them survive without their wings? They had both turned their backs on what they were. There would be no turning back from this.

*A.R. Johnston is a small-town girl from Nova Scotia, Canada. Her style of writing is considered Urban Fantasy. Her first major publication is part of an anthology called First Love and she has several more titles lined up. She is a lover of coffee, good tv shows, horror flicks, and reader of books. She pretends to be a writer when real life doesn't get in the way. Pesky full-time job and adulting!*

# Torn and Tattered
## by A.R. Johnston

They were both now torn, tattered and bloodied. They had made the decision to not return to either realm. They would live among the humans. To be together forevermore.

It was not something to be taken lightly, to rid themselves of all that made them what they were. They were savage in destroying the wings that had once been their shining glory. Their screams had filled the air. Feathers, bone, and blood sprayed through the air. Their once angelic and demon blood now flowed to seep into the ground below. Torn and tattered, breathing heavy, they left it all behind.

*A.R. Johnston is a small-town girl from Nova Scotia, Canada. Her style of writing is considered Urban Fantasy. Her first major publication is part of an anthology called First Love and she has several more titles lined up. She is a lover of coffee, good tv shows, horror flicks, and reader of books. She pretends to be a writer when real life doesn't get in the way. Pesky full-time job and adulting!*

# Defiance
## by A.R. Johnston

They were being hunted. They were what both realms feared the most. A pairing of both angelic and demon together. It wasn't done. They hadn't cared; it was worth all they had done to make it happen. There was not anything in either realm that could tear them apart now.

They may not have had long together—it had felt like a lifetime—in the end they had died in each other's arms, in defiance to all. They would not be torn asunder. Now stands a statue of them as a reminder to those that wish to do the same.

*A.R. Johnston is a small-town girl from Nova Scotia, Canada. Her style of writing is considered Urban Fantasy. Her first major publication is part of an anthology called First Love and she has several more titles lined up. She is a lover of coffee, good tv shows, horror flicks, and reader of books. She pretends to be a writer when real life doesn't get in the way. Pesky full-time job and adulting!*

# Lack of Faith
## by G. Allen Wilbanks

"Tell me, Father. How do you know when you have lost faith in God?"

Father Jacob sat in the confessional booth, listening to the shadowy figure behind the screen. He glanced at his watch, hoping this would not be another long, rambling session.

"I can't give you the answer to that, my son," he replied. "Only you know for certain, in your heart, the strength of your faith."

"No, not me, Father. I'm talking about your faith, not mine. I mean, what kind of priest can't keep a demon out of his own church?"

The smell of sulphur surrounded Jacob.

*G. Allen Wilbanks is a member of the Horror Writers Association (HWA) and has published over 50 short stories in various magazines and on-line venues. He is the author of two short story collections, and the novel, When Darkness Comes.*
*Website: www.gallenwilbanks.com*
*Blog: DeepDarkThoughts.com*

# The City of Angles
## by Gregg Cunningham

Zak smiled as he inhaled the joint, squinting as the smoke drifting into his eyes blinded him temporarily.

The tourist was laid out on her stomach, oblivious to the mess he was making on her back with the rusty ink gun.

*Fuck 'em!*

Sure, he could fuck her up and spell her tramp stamp the wrong way around, like all the summer tattoo artists done in the shop, but he was classier than that.

He liked to screw with them, send them off with something really special.

"All done. You wanna check it out?"

*I like to call it Hepatitis C.*

*Gregg Cunningham 48, short story writer who has had to pick up his game since stumbling into facebook writer's groups. He has stories published by 559 Publishing in in 13 Bites volume 3,4,5, Plan 9 from Outer space, Other Realms, Heard It on The Radio, 559 Ways to Die, short stories publishing by Zombie Pirate Publishing in Relationship add Vice, Full Metal Horror, Phuket Tattoo, World War four and Flash Fiction Addiction (flash) with Zombie Pirate Publishing, and also in Daastan Magazine Chapter 11 and Brian,Rich and the Wardrobe.*
*Amazon: www.amazon.com/-/e/B016OTHX0K*

# The End Justifies the Means
### by Carole de Monclin

"You've outdone yourself this time."

"What can I say? I love fire."

"The boss will be livid."

"He'll understand. Eventually."

"You burned one of His most significant symbols on Earth."

"Not completely. Besides, faith's in the heart, not in stones."

"Sophistry."

"Look at what I've accomplished. They're all united."

"That won't last."

"I've also exposed their hypocrisy. Pledging millions to rebuild an old pile when they abandon others to poverty."

"Notre Dame, an old pile?"

"Just wait. They'll amend their ways and flock back to Him. We'll see who the boss praises then."

"Who needs demons with angels like you?"

*Carole de Monclin* has lived in France and Australia, but for the moment the USA is home. She finds inspiration from her travels. She loves Science Fiction because it explores the human mind in a way no other genre can. Plus, who doesn't love spaceships and lasers? Her stories appear in the Exoplanet Magazine and Angels - A Dark Drabbles Anthology.
Website: CaroledeMonclin.com
Twitter: @CaroledeMonclin

# Evil Wins This Round
## by Sinister Sweetheart

Eae releases her pawn. "Your move, Abatu."

The entities survey the board; Abatu radiating fire, Eae a soothing tinkling of bells. Adversaries as old as time; playing an eternal game of chess with humanity.

Abatu moves his king to E4 with a sneer. Eae's eyes widen in surprise.

"Demon…it seems you're ahead. Time to reconvene at our posts, we'll pick back up tomorrow."

Abatu lets out a sinister cackle. "Aww, come on, Eae. You always call it quits when I start to win!"

A tear escapes the angel's eye; the world was in Abatu's hands for one more day.

*Since **Sinister Sweetheart** made her first post to a popular Internet forum, she's taken the horror community by storm. Her ability to create, terrify, and drive home her stories is insurmountable. Sinister Sweetheart's published works can be found in multiple anthologies for all to read, but be forewarned, if you do... you may want to call your therapist after, her stories are terrifying, disturbing and devilishly unsettling. She is not only a fright visually, but also has a creepy tentacle in horror podcasting as well. Sinister Sweetheart writes, voice acts and is the media director of the Scarecrow Tales podcast.*
*Website: Sinistersweetheart.wixsite.com/sinistersweetheart*
*Facebook: NMBrownStories*

# Angel Gloating
## by Olivia Arieti

The blade was gleaming before his eyes, a lugubrious sheen that was driving him mad. What was he waiting for? That damned good angel was pleading, while his hellish partner kept shouting, "Hurry, Dan! Plunge it in."

No reason he shouldn't; the bastard had totally ruined him.

The good angel's translucent hand was now on his, the demon's one on his shoulder; both pressing and demanding.

Dan's heart and mind were fighting desperately when an atrocious pain made him fall on his victim's body and the knife penetrated the heart.

His final glance saw both angels rejoice and swiftly depart.

*Olivia Arieti has a degree from the University of Pisa and lives in Torre del Lago Puccini, Italy, with her family. Besides being a published playwright, she loves writing retellings of fairy tales, and at the same time is intrigued by supernatural and horror themes. Her stories appeared in several magazines and anthologies like Enchanted Conversations, Enchanted Tales Literary Magazine, Fantasia Divinity Magazine, Cliterature, Medieval Nightmares, Static Movement, 100 Doors To Madness Forgotten Tomb Press, Black Cats Horrified Press, Bloody Ghost Stories Full Moon Books, Death And Decorations Thirteen O'Clock Press, Infective Ink, Pandemonium Press, Pussy Magic Magazine.*

# The Battle of Galmore
## by J.D. Bell

Men sing of the great battle of Galmore. Of a time when the Lord of the Dark Mountain sent hordes of ogres and goblins to drive mankind from the plains. When terrible beasts poured down from the mountain. An army mortal men could not defeat.

Men prayed to the Goddess of Light for their salvation. Hearing their cries, the goddess sent her army of angels on winged chariots. The battle raged for the passing of twelve moons. The savage beasts driven into pits of fire.

In honour, generations of men sing songs of the great victory of angels over evil.

*J.D. Bell is an award-winning, internationally published, author of flash fiction and short stories. He recently retired from the world of writing advertising copy and is now enjoying the universe of creative fiction.*
*Facebook: jim.writes.stories*
*Twitter: @JimBell58*

# The Scarlet Winged Angel
by Pamela Jeffs

A landscape scarred with fire and decay. Such a waste. I fold my wings back to my shoulders and glide toward Earth. Time to end this.

A crowd of humans clusters at the gates of a ruined church. They are withered creatures, mewling plaintively for mercy. As I land they turn, each and every one with eyes full of hope. "Are you here to save us, Angel?" asks one matron, a suitcase held in her hand.

"No," says another, a grandfather, hair white as snow. "She comes to take us to Hell. Look at her wings. They're red, not white."

*Pamela Jeffs is a speculative fiction author living in Queensland, Australia with her husband and two daughters. She is a member of the Queensland Writers' Centre and has had numerous short fiction pieces published in recent national and international anthologies. In 2017 and again in 2018, Pamela was nominated for an Australian Aurealis Award in the category of 'Best Science Fiction Short Story'. Her debut collection titled 'Red Hour and Other Strange Tales' was released in March 2018.*
*Website: www.pamelajeffs.com*
*Facebook: pamelajeffsauthor*

# Deal Me In
## by Jo Seysener

"You in?"

"Yeah, let 'em rip."

"Souls?"

"I got Trump."

They both giggled, a high sound unbefitting their ranks. Long fingers, pale as death laid cards upon the marble. The crypt was cold, but then so was the body.

Malice licked his maw, tongue snaking out to taste the soul.

"Raise."

"What?"

"A feather."

"A bent one. I can't have you taking my best."

"Done."

"Call."

"Ah, ye bugger."

The angel smiled, sweeping his arm across the sealed tomb.

A breeze slipped across the cold stone, raising the spirit. Slight and purple it sighted the angel's sly smile and screamed.

*Jo Seysener is a mum of three crazies, a scatter of chickens, a decrepit kelpie and a rambunctious GSD. She lives with her husband near Brisbane, Australia. When she is not exposing her kids to cult story books from her childhood, she can be found in the kitchen experimenting with new flavours and pairings. She adores alpacas.*
*Facebook: joseysener*
*Website: www.joseysener.com*

# Shepherding
## by Cecelia Hopkins-Drewer

The angel stood facing the zombies. They were ugly creatures.

"Who let you out?" he said.

"Urg," replied the zombies.

"Back, back, back through the gate," Rafael stormed.

The zombies were like sheep; they shuffled in the direction Raphael indicated.

"You sent them the wrong way," Parpiel said. His honest white face shone with innocence.

"Oh, did I?" Raphael said. He was confused. He ushered the zombies in the other direction where they would ultimately feed upon human flesh. "There you go."

Parpiel threw off his mask of light. "You white angels are so dim," he chortled. "You always obey."

*Cecelia Hopkins-Drewer is a speculative fiction writer, poet and scholar, who lives in Adelaide, South Australia. She has also written a Masters paper on H.P. Lovecraft, and a teenage vampire series that commences with "Mystic Evermore". Her science fiction poetry has been published in "The Mentor" a fanzine edited by Ron Clarke.*
*Amazon: amazon.com/Cecelia-Hopkins-Drewer/e/B071G968NM*

# From the Ashes
## by Jem McCusker

The flame of resistance was an omen of change, for when burnt out, from its ashes an angel will rise.

Will it be from the white abyss, with feathers gleaming and a halo bright? Or a fallen legend, of strength and darkness with demon blood?

In the shadows I stand, biding my time, for in ashes rested a new life will dawn. My chains are stilled, my mouth still gagged, I wait in the hopes a heavenly saviour from above will release my soul. A chill stills the room, a hand appears, black wicked nails, I'm doomed, as I feared.

*Jem McCusker is a middle grade fiction author, living near Brisbane with her two sons and husband. Her first book Stone Guardians the Rise of Eden was released in 2018 and she is working on the sequel. She is releasing a Novella for the Four Quills writing group, A Storm of Wind and Rain series in July, 2019. She longs to be a full-time author, won't wear yellow and loves rabbits. Follow Jem on Twitter, Facebook and Instagram. Details on her website.*
*Website: www.jemmccusker.com*

# The Guardian's Last Stand
## by Kelly A. Harmon

"I shouldn't." Buck eyed the slope, pushing his snowboard back and forth with one toe.

The thought had come more and more lately; he wondered if he were losing his nerve.

Buck's guardian angel—one feather left in the sad remnants of his once glorious wings—tried again. "I shouldn't do this," he whispered in Buck's ear.

The demon smirked. "Coward," it said in the other.

Buck leapt, breaking records as he flew across the snow.

Then, his board struck a buried tree. Buck cartwheeled, landing in a bloodied heap with his guardian angel.

A single brilliant feather wafted downward.

*Kelly A. Harmon* *is an award-winning journalist and author, and a member of the Science Fiction & Fantasy Writers of America and Horror Writers of America. A Baltimore native, she writes the Charm City Darkness series. The fourth book in the series, In the Eye of the Beholder, is now available. Find her short fiction in many magazines and anthologies, including Occult Detective Quarterly; Terra! Tara! Terror! and Deep Cuts: Mayhem, Menace and Misery. Website: kellyaharmon.com*
*Twitter: @kellyaharmon*

# Salvation
## by R.A. Goli

Lucette lay slumped against the concrete wall, praying for her angel. Her dark t-shirt glistened, as blood seeped through the cloth from her wound. The knife wielder had long since disappeared with her purse.

A shadow loomed and a shard of fear pierced her heart. She saw the large feathered wings as they spread out, felt a soft breeze as they flapped. The angel stood over her.

He held out his hand. As soon as she took it, her pain eased.

"Thank you," she whispered.

The Angel of Death wrapped her within his soft, black wings and she was gone.

*R.A. Goli is an Australian writer of horror, fantasy, and speculative short stories. In addition to writing, her interests include reading, gaming, the occasional walk, and annoying her dog, two cats, and husband. Check out her numerous publications including her fantasy novella, The Eighth Dwarf, and her collection of short stories, Unfettered;*
*Website: ragoliauthor.wordpress.com*
*Facebook: RAGoliAuthor*

# Closure
## by Liam Hogan

He leaned against the apartment door, heard it click. Closing tired eyes, he listened to the rumble of arguments above and below, soft sobs, frantic sex. Further away, gunshots.

***

"Is it done?"

"Almost."

"Almost?"

"Before you draw a line under their existence, you must live among them."

"For how long?"

"As long as it takes."

***

On the bed—the only piece of furniture—lay the book. All he had to do was close it.

He missed his wings. Missed a hell of a lot of other things besides. But most of all his wings.

Maybe one more day.

Maybe tomorrow.

*Liam Hogan* is a London based short story writer, the host of Liars' League, and a Ministry of Stories mentor. His story "Ana", appears in Best of British Science Fiction 2016 (NewCon Press) and his twisted fantasy collection, "Happy Ending Not Guaranteed", is published by Arachne Press. Website: happyendingnotguaranteed.blogspot.co.uk Twitter: @LiamJHogan

# Nahaliel
## by Vonnie Winslow Crist

Warned about flood potential, county roads inspector Elmer Cheney decided Deer Creek wasn't a priority. When it overflowed its banks, swallowed Rocks Road, he begrudgingly returned to the site. He saw Deer Creek had also flooded a field—leaving cows and calves stranded.

The farmer waved at Elmer for help.

Elmer shook his head. He didn't care about cattle.

Suddenly, Angel Nahaliel, who presides over streams, appeared as a passerby, waded into water to help mothers and calves escape a watery death.

Then, Nahaliel called forth a surge which washed Elmer into the torrent.

"Karma," said Nahaliel as Elmer drowned.

*Vonnie Winslow Crist is author of The Enchanted Dagger, Owl Light, The Greener Forest, Murder on Marawa Prime, and other award-winning books. Her fiction is included in "Amazing Stories," "Cast of Wonders," "Outposts of Beyond," Killing It Softly 2, Defending the Future - Dogs of War, Midnight Masquerade, Chaos of Hard Clay, and elsewhere. A cloverhand who has found so many four-leafed clovers she keeps them in jars, Vonnie strives to celebrate the power of myth in her writing.*
*Website: www.vonniewinslowcrist.com*

# Choose Your Own Ending
## by Alice Lam

"Please don't. Please, just listen to me," she screams.

"Shut up." You shove her back in her seat. You feel strangely calm as you accelerate through the final chicane. Then you sharply turn the steering wheel and the Jeep fishtails towards a large gap in the crash barrier.

She's getting louder now. "I didn't mean it, Amy. He's all yours. I'm sorry."

Not long to go. Do you say that out loud?

You allow yourself a quick glance; your sister, hands bound in her lap.

Your foot hovers over the brake.

In three seconds, you could be good or bad.

*Alice Lam has loved writing for as long as she remembers. Her story 'Lilies' came fifth out of 258 entries in the Atlantis Short Story Competition 2017/18 and was published in Atlantis' first anthology in October 2018. She has another two short stories published in Didcot Writers' anthologies – 'The Bright Side' and "Facing The Music" and a fourth awaiting publication. You can read some of her short stories, writing blogs, plus links to her beta reading / critique and health writer services on her website.*
*Website: www.alicelambooks.com*

# Sins of the Fathers
## by Alexander Pyles

They did not give us wings; instead aspirations that we could one day rule the sky. Our thirst for dominion dogged us as we conquered and fought. There were none to stand before us, until the Fathers came to humble us.

They flew on wings of fire, bearing weapons forged in thunder. We were unprepared and unwilling to fight those who had given us life. Yet, when our bodies piled high and our blood ran like rivers over the fields, our choice was made.

We would build airships and invade the Father's halls, take their weapons, and extinguish their wings.

*Alexander Pyles resides in IL with his wife and children. He holds an MA in Philosophy and an MFA in Writing Popular Fiction. His short story chapbook titled, "Milo (01001101 01101001 01101100 01101111)," from Radix Media, is due out fall 2019. His other short fiction has appeared on 101fiction.org, River and South Review, and other venues.
Website: www.pylesofbooks.com
Twitter: @Pylesofbooks*

# She Comes with the Dawn
## by Adam Bennett

Sweeping wings of gold and ivory brush against my face and I know that no man has stood this close before. The shining golden armour, the flowing hair and majestic wings allow no mistake. I am standing mere inches from an honest to God angel. Am I dead? Am I dreaming? I have no idea. She speaks, a glowing, pulsating stream of golden light escaping from within her open mouth, but I cannot understand. She is waiting on a reply, but I know not the question.

A shining golden sword sweeps from behind the angel, striking down with great vengeance.

*Seven billion years ago an O Class star exploded in the distant reaches of the Virgo Supercluster. Over the course of eons, particles of the star's dust spread through the universe until finally a series of them coalesced in New South Wales, Australia during the mid eighties. Thus was born the author and publisher* **Adam Bennett**. *His writing shows his yearning to return to his rightful home among the stars, a wish he will achieve, even if he has to wait until the heat death of the universe.*
*Website: zombiepiratepublishing.com*
*Facebook: adambennettauthor*

# Bullies
## by Gabriella Balcom

Leaning on her cane, the old, hunchbacked woman slowly walked down the sidewalk. But she swayed as if she'd fall over when a rock hit her back.

Jami and Wanda laughed, pelting her with more stones.

"That's not funny." Nellie ran up to her mean classmates. "She could fall and get hurt."

"Who cares?" Jami retorted. Wanda knelt for another missile.

Nellie knocked it from her hand. "You wouldn't like stuff thrown at you."

The bullies sneered, then walked away.

"Are you okay?" Nellie asked the old woman.

She nodded and replied, "Your parents must be very proud of you."

*Gabriella Balcom lives in Texas with her family, loves reading and writing, and thinks she was born with a book in her hands. She works in a mental health field, and writes fantasy, horror/thriller, romance, children's stories, and sci-fi. She likes travelling, music, good shows, photography, history, interesting tales, and animals. Gabriella says she's a sucker for a great story and loves forests, mountains, and back roads which might lead who knows where. She has a weakness for lasagne, garlic bread, tacos, cheese, and chocolate, but not necessarily in that order.*
*Facebook: GabriellaBalcom.lonestarauthor*

# Little One
## by Jem McCusker

"Ten-year-old female, snake bite." Voices rushed by around me.

I lay on the hard ambulance bed at the emergency entry. My mother weeps, my father's legs give out. No hands are there to catch him.

The tall man at the end of the bed holds my attention with his warm smile and neatly pressed white uniform. "Hello."

"Hi." I try to wave but my arm won't lift, instead it shivers with cold.

"You're in safe hands little one."

My eyes feel heavy, his image begins to blur and shine.

"Close your eyes and take my hands. It's time, little one."

*Jem McCusker is a middle grade fiction author, living near Brisbane with her two sons and husband. Her first book Stone Guardians the Rise of Eden was released in 2018 and she is working on the sequel. She is releasing a Novella for the Four Quills writing group, A Storm of Wind and Rain series in July, 2019. She longs to be a full-time author, won't wear yellow and loves rabbits. Follow Jem on Twitter, Facebook and Instagram. Details on her website. Website: www.jemmccusker.com*

# Guardian of Who?
## by Alexander Pyles

"What's that thing on your shoulder?"

"It's my guardian angel."

Louis rubbed his eyes. "Are you sure it's an angel?"

"Yeah, why wouldn't it be? Do you know what angels look like?"

"No, but I don't think they would look like that. Where did it come from?"

"He appeared one day."

"Does it talk?" Louis leaned in, but I could feel the angel draw back. After a minute he said, "Well, I think it's an overgrown bat," and turned away.

I wanted to say something, but my angel tickled my ear and a sharp talon pricked as it whispered, "Kill."

*Alexander Pyles resides in IL with his wife and children. He holds an MA in Philosophy and an MFA in Writing Popular Fiction. His short story chapbook titled, "Milo (01001101 01101001 01101100 01101111)," from Radix Media, is due out fall 2019. His other short fiction has appeared on 101fiction.org, River and South Review, and other venues. Website: www.pylesofbooks.com Twitter: @Pylesofbooks*

# Grounded
## by Patrick Winters

The vagrant stirred in his spot between the dumpsters, a soft cooing bringing him back to full and wretched consciousness. He looked down to see a dove pecking at his worn boots.

He regarded it for a moment, then reached out, grabbing hold and pulling it up to his chest without a single squawk of protest.

"I had wings once, too," he whispered to it. "They were glorious."

His hand wrapped around the bird's head. He twisted—hard—and smirked at the tiny snap.

"But no more."

He held it awhile more, feeling closer to his Father than ever before.

*Patrick Winters* is a graduate of Illinois College in Jacksonville, IL, where he earned a Bachelor of Arts degree in English Literature and Creative Writing and achieved membership into Sigma Tau Delta, an international English honors society. Winters is now a proud member of the Horror Writers Association, and his work has been published in the likes of Sanitarium Magazine, Deadman's Tome, Trysts of Fate, and other such titles. A full list of his previous publications may be found at his author's site. Website: wintersauthor.azurewebsites.net/Publications/List

# Tough Decisions
## by Alanah Andrews

Shutting the door firmly, the president leant against the wall.

"It's the right decision," said the angel hovering above his shoulder.

"Go away." President Montreal swatted at the air behind him.

"Haven't I always looked out for you?" The angel followed the president across the office. "Who helped you get into office? Made sure you were elected?"

The president ran a hand through his grey hair.

"Attack first," hissed the angel. "That's the only way to protect our country."

President Montreal nodded. "I suppose you're right."

The angel smiled and adjusted his halo, making sure it was covering his horns.

*Alanah Andrews* writes speculative fiction and spends far too much time debating whether 1984 or The Handmaid's Tale are most representative of our future. Her YA dystopian novel about a future where emotions are forbidden, Eve of Eridu, was released in 2018. She has also had several short stories published in a range of different places. When she's not writing, Alanah runs the Australian Speculative Fiction group, teaches high school English, and attempts to raise two children. She has a husky, a pony, a blue-tongue lizard, and dreams of travelling Australia in a bus.
Website: www.alanahandrews.com
Facebook: alanahandrewsauthor

# Handle with Care
## by G. Allen Wilbanks

"I don't want to go," said the angel.

The archangel shook his head. "None of us do, but it's your turn to go down and work as a guardian."

"How long before I can come back?"

"I don't know," the archangel shrugged. "However long it takes. Usually fifty or a hundred years."

The angel left the room, shoulders slumped. After only a few minutes, he wandered back in.

"You're still here?" asked the archangel.

"I just got back. I went down, but it was already over when I got there. Nobody warned me that humans could be so incredibly fragile."

*G. Allen Wilbanks is a member of the Horror Writers Association (HWA) and has published over 50 short stories in various magazines and on-line venues. He is the author of two short story collections, and the novel, When Darkness Comes.*
*Website: www.gallenwilbanks.com*
*Blog: DeepDarkThoughts.com*

# My Child
## by R.G. Halstead

The troubled teenage girl sat and waited. She desperately needed to talk to the man of God. He would guide her through this problem. A gentle, kind man.

Entering the room, Reverend Smith smiled. Before he even sat down, she sighed and then whimpered, "I keep hearing voices, Reverend Smith. Telling me what to do. Who should I listen to? The demon voices? Or the angel voices?"

Rubbing his large hands together, he sat down beside the pretty young thing. Close. Massaging her shoulders and then down towards her breasts, he replied, "You listen to me, my child. Just me."

*R.G. Halstead, a 63-year-old, takes to writing late in his life. Influences? Those old Alfred Hitchcock Mystery Magazines from the late 1950s and the 1960s with the great twisty endings. Love them.*

# New Eden
## by Rich Rurshell

As the angel had instructed, we distributed the wax amongst those of us taking refuge in the valley. As far as we knew, the disease had turned the rest of humanity into bloodthirsty savages.

The *corrupt* we called them.

We stuffed the wax into our ears as hordes of the corrupt descended into the valley.

We wept as the angel burst into song, his heavenly voice audible, even through the wax. The corrupt fell to the ground, their ears bleeding, dead.

A star appeared above us.

"Others like you will come," said the angel.

We were standing in New Eden.

*Rich Rurshell is a short story writer from Suffolk, England. Rich writes Horror, Sci-Fi, and Fantasy, and his stories can be found in various short story anthologies and magazines. Most recently, his story "Subject: Galilee" was published in World War Four from Zombie Pirate Publishing, and "Life Choices" was published in Salty Tales from Stormy Island Publishing. When Rich is not writing stories, he likes to write and perform music.*
*Facebook: richrurshellauthor*

# Colour Code
## by Sinister Sweetheart

When Lucifer plummeted from Heaven, Hell came into creation. This started an eternal struggle between good and evil. No one mentions smaller battles, the first being over colour.

Lucifer warped the world's colours to cast influence on humans. He loved black and red best. Red for blood; of life leaving the body. Red for danger; saying STOP. Black for Death; despair, hopelessness of the spirit.

God had two. White for purity of soul, hope, the cleansing of spirit. Light blue for peace and enlightenment. When people look up to the Heavens, he wants them to see a clear blue sky.

*Since **Sinister Sweetheart** made her first post to a popular Internet forum, she's taken the horror community by storm. Her ability to create, terrify, and drive home her stories is insurmountable. Sinister Sweetheart's published works can be found in multiple anthologies for all to read, but be forewarned, if you do... you may want to call your therapist after, her stories are terrifying, disturbing and devilishly unsettling. She is not only a fright visually, but also has a creepy tentacle in horror podcasting as well. Sinister Sweetheart writes, voice acts and is the media director of the Scarecrow Tales podcast.*
*Website: Sinistersweetheart.wixsite.com/sinistersweetheart*
*Facebook: NMBrownStories*

# Angel Leaves
## by Ximena Escobar

Angel pulled herself up, clenching the edge of the window. Her shoe slipped off, but she trapped it against the wall; she could see her yellow star-lights gliding across her ceiling; one more push, and she'd be over the sill.

An odd gush of wind swept through her.

Leaning on the sill, she saw her shoe on the grass below, and threads of her hair appearing alongside her flaccid arm. She looked away in horror; but enormous energy tore through her startled heart, stretching her soul like sun rays.

The earth descended and the eternal sky lifted her like water.

*Ximena Escobar is an emerging author of literary fiction and poetry. Originally from Chile, she is the author of a translation into Spanish of the Broadway Musical "The Wizard of Oz", and of an original adaptation of the same, "Navidad en Oz". Clarendon House Publications published her first short story in the UK, "The Persistence of Memory", and Literally Stories her first online publication with "The Green Light". She has since had several acceptances from other publishers and is working very hard exploring new exciting avenues in her writing.*
*She lives in Nottingham with her family.*
*Facebook: Ximenautora*

# Brotherly Love
## by K.T. Tate

I miss my twin most of all. We had such a bond, such love, but now I have to fight just to get his attention.

Today's war is poor little Julie, so young and faithful. I arch her back, racking her body as my words fill her mouth with obscenities for the priest. I dare him, scowling, burning this body as they throw their holy water.

Finally, he does it. He invokes the angels to protect her, invokes Zephiel. Light, unseen by mortal eyes, awes me. It burns, she writhes, and I smile as I watch my glorious brother descend.

*K.T. Tate lives in Cambridgeshire in the UK. She writes mainly weird fiction, cosmic horror and strange monster stories.*
*Website: eldritchhollow.wordpress.com*
*Tumblr: eldritch-hollow.tumblr.com*

# Guardians
## by Alanah Andrews

"Which one's yours?"

We peer down from the clouds, and I point out a man in jeans and a black shirt.

"Not bad," says Lucinda.

"Not bad? He's hopeless. I'm constantly saving him."

Her eyes are dreamy. "I meant, not bad to look at."

My stomach plummets. I stretch my wings to their full spread and murmur something non-committal.

"Raphael!" Her blue eyes widen.

My spirits rise. "Listen—"

"Your charge. Watch out!"

Too late, the human I'm supposed to protect is reduced to a bloody pulp.

Lucinda retches.

"I guess this is a bad time to ask you out?"

***Alanah Andrews*** *writes speculative fiction and spends far too much time debating whether 1984 or The Handmaid's Tale are most representative of our future. Her YA dystopian novel about a future where emotions are forbidden, Eve of Eridu, was released in 2018. She has also had several short stories published in a range of different places. When she's not writing, Alanah runs the Australian Speculative Fiction group, teaches high school English, and attempts to raise two children. She has a husky, a pony, a blue-tongue lizard, and dreams of travelling Australia in a bus.*
*Website: www.alanahandrews.com*
*Facebook: alanahandrewsauthor*

# God's Messenger
## by J. Farrington

The world rejoiced when the angel appeared on the mountain top. A brilliant light emanated from her that could be seen far and wide. People from all over travelled to be in her presence, although she never spoke, they claimed to be enlightened just by being next to her.

Then it happened, she opened her mouth and called for silence. Instantly, the World stood still.

Was this a message straight from God? Was this his divine will for mankind? In truth, nobody knew what to expect.

One thing is for sure, nobody wished for her next words.

"God is dead…"

*J. Farrington is an aspiring author from the West Midlands, UK. His genre of choice is horror; whether that be psychological, suspense, supernatural or straight up weird, he'll give it a shot! He has loved writing from a young age but has only publicly been spreading his darker thoughts and sinister imagination via social platforms since 2018. If you would like to view his previous work, or merely lurk in the shadows...watching, you can keep up to date with future projects by spirit board or alternatively, the following;*
*Twitter: @SurvivorTrench*
*Reddit: TrenchChronicles*

# Nathaniel
## by Vonnie Winslow Crist

"Save us," prayed seven honourable men as they were tossed into flames by King Jair's degree.

The angel Nathaniel, lord over the element of fire, appeared in a blaze of wings. "Fear not," said Nathaniel as he raised his pale as ice hands and extinguished the flames.

"Hush. Rise, then leave this place," ordered the angel when the seven men fell to their knees and expressed their gratitude.

They witnessed the fury in his burning eyes and fled in fear.

Next, Nathaniel called forth a fire storm, incinerated King Jair, plus one thousand of his followers. Then, the angel smiled.

*Vonnie Winslow Crist is author of The Enchanted Dagger, Owl Light, The Greener Forest, Murder on Marawa Prime, and other award-winning books. Her fiction is included in "Amazing Stories," "Cast of Wonders," "Outposts of Beyond," Killing It Softly 2, Defending the Future - Dogs of War, Midnight Masquerade, Chaos of Hard Clay, and elsewhere. A cloverhand who has found so many four-leafed clovers she keeps them in jars, Vonnie strives to celebrate the power of myth in her writing.*
*Website: www.vonniewinslowcrist.com*

# The God-Killer
## by Shelly Jarvis

When the humans revolted, Father rejoiced, delighted they finally understood free will. When they created a portal to Heaven without his help, he was amazed by their ingenuity. When they showed him their god-killer, the weapon that had already slain six other deities, he knew fear for the first time in his eternal life.

They killed him.

We're fighting back, but we're losing. The forces of Heaven and Hell are no match for them. Our little brothers grew up while we bickered with one another.

Tomorrow is the seventh day since they killed Father. All I want is to rest.

*Shelly Jarvis is a speculative fiction author from West Virginia, US. She found a life-long love of sci-fi and fantasy in the 3rd grade when she found Madeleine L'Engle's "A Wrinkle in Time." Shelly is an avid reader, a Whovian, the ideal viewer of dog rescue videos, and undoubtedly Ravenclaw. She currently has two YA sci-fi books available for purchase on Amazon.*
*Website: www.ShellyJarvis.com*

# Crossed Wires
## by J. Farrington

For millennia they retrieved the souls of those who passed, guiding them on their journey. The work of the Divine and all who is Holy, or so they thought. Never passing judgement, merely aiding the transition to their afterlife. If only one of them had asked the questions, the questions burning in the back of their minds.

Where are they sending them? Why do they resist when the ground opens before them? And why have they never been permitted into paradise themselves?

If only they had asked whether they were Angels sent from Heaven…

Or the demons sent from Hell.

*J. Farrington is an aspiring author from the West Midlands, UK. His genre of choice is horror; whether that be psychological, suspense, supernatural or straight up weird, he'll give it a shot! He has loved writing from a young age but has only publicly been spreading his darker thoughts and sinister imagination via social platforms since 2018. If you would like to view his previous work, or merely lurk in the shadows...watching, you can keep up to date with future projects by spirit board or alternatively, the following;*
*Twitter: @SurvivorTrench*
*Reddit: TrenchChronicles*

# Sins and Virtues
## by Henry Herz

The seven Deadly Sins lounged along a flawless ebony table. The Contrary Virtues stood across from them in balance.

"We are just as important to God's plan as you!" Pride yelled at Humility.

"How so?" asked Abstinence. "You do not feed the hungry, shelter the homeless, nor clothe the naked."

Lust giggled. "She said 'naked'!"

"Really?"

"Abbie needs to get laid," suggested Lust. "I volunteer."

"Abbie's a dolt!" shouted Anger. "We Deadly Sins give mortal lives meaning."

"You bring nothing but misery," replied Patience.

"Fool! It is only through their lifelong struggle for self-control that humans reach their full potential."

*__Henry Herz__ edited the dark fantasy anthology, BEYOND THE PALE, featuring stories by Saladin Ahmed, Peter Beagle, Heather Brewer, Jim Butcher, Rachel Caine, Kami Garcia, Nancy Holder, and Jane Yolen. His horror story, Gluttony, will appear in the anthology, CLASSICS REMIXED. He authored the children's books: MONSTER GOOSE NURSERY RHYMES, WHEN YOU GIVE AN IMP A PENNY, MABEL & THE QUEEN OF DREAMS, LITTLE RED CUTTLEFISH, CAP'N REX & HIS CLEVER CREW, HOW THE SQUID GOT TWO LONG ARMS, ALICE'S MAGIC GARDEN, GOOD EGG AND BAD APPLE, TWO PIRATES + ONE ROBOT, THE MAGIC SPATULA, and I AM SMOKE.*
*Website: www.henryherz.com*

# In Trouble
## by Wondra Vanian

Sally Peterson was a good little girl. The best. A faithful, God-fearing girl. When she swore an angel did...*things* to her, the adults were broken-hearted. It wasn't that they didn't believe her—but children were so easily deceived.

Though, in truth, there was no deceit. It was an angel. And he *did* do those things. But not all angels come from above.

They thought Sally was in trouble when they found her sobbing and bloody in her room. When her stomach began to swell. When she went into labour.

They didn't know what real trouble was until he was reborn.

*Wondra Vanian is an American living in the United Kingdom with her Welsh husband and their army of fur babies. A writer first, Wondra is also an avid gamer, photographer, cinephile, and blogger. She has music in her blood, sleeps with the lights on, and has been known to dance naked in the moonlight. Wondra was a multiple Top-Ten finisher in the 2017 and 2018 Preditors and Editors Reader's Poll, including ithe Best Author category. Her story, "Halloween Night," was named a Notable Contender for the Bristol Short Story Prize in 2015.*
*Website: www.wondravanian.com*

# Pride
## by Cecelia Hopkins-Drewer

Lamiel jumped off the rooftop and landed with catlike grace. He was secure in the belief his prey was trapped, but it bounded away.

Lamiel reached forward, dropping into a crouch and stabbing with his spear. Once again, the weapon met empty air. The prey was cunning.

The prey feinted towards him with unexpected boldness. Lameil stepped back instinctively, not realising he was stepping into a noose.

The rope tightened around his ankle; it was made of steel strong enough to hold an angel. A bulldozer rolled forward threateningly. Lamiel could not die, but he could feel the awful pain.

*Cecelia Hopkins-Drewer is a speculative fiction writer, poet and scholar, who lives in Adelaide, South Australia. She has also written a Masters paper on H.P. Lovecraft, and a teenage vampire series that commences with "Mystic Evermore". Her science fiction poetry has been published in "The Mentor" a fanzine edited by Ron Clarke.*
*Amazon: amazon.com/Cecelia-Hopkins-Drewer/e/B071G968NM*

# One Breath Away from Death
## by E.L. Giles

"Help me," murmured the dying soldier, one breath away from death. "God, help me."

Who could hear him, he wondered, among all the moans and whimpers echoing eerily across the barren land?

He heard footsteps approaching. Finally, he wasn't alone. The soldier raised a weak arm, signalling his presence.

A luminous shape materialised over him. Beams of light radiated from his perfect white skin. He flapped his immense golden wings several times before folding them.

"Everything is all right," said the angel, crouching. He took the dying man in his arms, soothing him. "In a moment, everything will be over."

*E.L. Giles is a dreamer, passionate about art, a restless worker and a bit of a weird human. He started his artistic journey as a music composer until the need to put his thoughts and stories down on paper grew too strong for him to resist it any longer. He lives in the French Province of Quebec, Canada, with his girlfriend and two boys.*
*Facebook: elgilesauthor*
*Website: www.elgilesauthor.com*

# Who Tempts Whom?
## by Kelly A. Harmon

The demon, Pournelle, genuflected beside the pew and crossed himself—waiting for lightning to strike. When none came, he knelt and prayed, "Lord, I'm here to ask—"

"You'll never enter Heaven." Saint Michael appeared, fingering his blazing sword.

Pournelle recognised the blade for what it was; knew he had more power in his left hand than God had graced Michael with the sword.

He was tempted to prove it.

Pournelle lifted his eyes to the ceiling. "You blame the devil for temptation, Lord, but I'm not rising to the bait."

He snapped his fingers and disappeared. Tomorrow, he would try again.

*Kelly A. Harmon is an award-winning journalist and author, and a member of the Science Fiction & Fantasy Writers of America and Horror Writers of America. A Baltimore native, she writes the Charm City Darkness series. The fourth book in the series, In the Eye of the Beholder, is now available. Find her short fiction in many magazines and anthologies, including Occult Detective Quarterly; Terra! Tara! Terror! and Deep Cuts: Mayhem, Menace and Misery. Website: kellyaharmon.com*
*Twitter: @kellyaharmon*

# The Dealer
## by Aditya Deshmukh

My wife lay in my lap, snoring. With trembling hands, I reached for her wedding ring.

I gently lifted her head off my lap and kept it on a cushion.

I ran.

Kick-starting my second-hand scooter, I called my dealer.

He waited in a dark alley. Parking my scooter outside, I nodded at him. He approached me. I showed him the ring.

"Looks like a woman's. Last time it was yours. This time your wife's, eh?"

"Quick, give me my drugs."

He placed the ring on my palm and closed my fingers around it. "That's all the drug you need."

*Aditya Deshmukh is a mechanical engineering student who likes exploring the mechanics of writing as much as he likes tinkering with machines. He writes dark fiction and poetry. He is published in over three dozen anthologies and has a poetry book "Opium Hearts" and a collection of drabbles coming out soon. He likes chatting with people who share similar interests, so feel free to check him out.*
*Facebook: adityadeshmukhwrites*
*Website: www.adityadeshmukh.com*

# Last Moments
## by Eddie D. Moore

The beeps coming from the heart monitor slowed. Joe turned unfocused eyes in his wife's direction and said weakly, "Angels are in the room."

A tear dropped from Mary's cheek. "That's a good thing. Can you describe them?"

"I can't look directly at their faces, but they're wearing white robes and carrying silver spears." A touch of confusion entered Joe's voice. "They move around like they're afraid of something."

"They're probably just excited."

Joe's heartbeat increased rapidly. "Another just ran into the room. Something dark is chasing him." He gasped. "The spears aren't enough."

The monitor emitted a single tone.

*Eddie D. Moore travels extensively for work, and he spends much of that time listening to audio books. The rest of the time is spent dreaming of stories to write and he spends the weekends writing them. His stories have been published by Jouth Webzine, Kzine, Alien Dimensions, Theme of Absence, Devolution Z, and Fantasia Divinity Magazine.*
*Website: eddiedmoore.wordpress.com*

# Fallen
## by C.L. Williams

Leanne stopped Penn from doing the regrettable. He knew she could not be human, and she eventually revealed her angel wings. Penn was thankful but some of Leanne's actions soon felt too ambiguous for someone who is supposedly an angel. Penn doesn't know any other angels and ignores his intuition, regardless of how loud it is in his head.

Leanne one day asks Penn, "Will you follow me anywhere?"

He reluctantly replies, "I will." Before he knows it, Leanne reveals the facade that her wings are black and she's a fallen. Penn is now condemned to Hell for all eternity.

*C.L. Williams is an independent author from central Virginia. He has written eight poetry books, four novellas, one novel, and a contributor to multiple anthologies, with the most recent appearance being an all-ages anthology titled Temoli from Thazbook. His most recent poetry book, The Paradox Complex, features the poem "Sad Crying Clown" that is now a video on YouTube directed by Matthew Mark Hunter of MMH Productions. C.L. Williams is currently working on his first sci-fi book, an all-ages book titled Novo: Away from Earth. When not writing, C.L. Williams is reading and sharing the work of other independent authors.*
*Facebook: writer434*
*Twitter: @writer_434*

# The Big Hit
## by Michael Balletti

When Azazel and his crew told me the plan, I knew it was either join or die. And I've always been a survivor.

The big guy had been pissing people off for a while. It was really just a matter of time. I'm sure he knew it, too.

He was nearly gone by the time I got there, but I had to get my sword dirty. Just part of the deal.

But it's chaos down here. The infighting has already begun. And who knows what's going to happen once the guy upstairs finds out we snuffed out the morning star.

*Michael Balletti lives in New Jersey. His work has appeared in Drabbledark: An Anthology of Dark Drabbles, Nothing's Sacred: Vol. 4, Scifaikuest, Theme of Absence and 200 CCs, among others.*

# High Treason
## by Stephanie Scissom

Lucifer fished for his cigarettes, his pose deliberately casual.

"What are you doing here, Gabriel? Am I the only place that you've left to go?"

"I come as an ally. Together, we can defeat Michael."

Lucifer laughed. "You? Go against Michael?"

"Heaven is terrible since the war. He's a tyrant."

Lucifer's boots made a slapping sound when they hit the ground. Gabriel flinched.

"You murdered my children."

"It wasn't me!"

"DO NOT LIE TO ME!" Lucifer roared and threw Gabriel against the wall.

Lucifer glanced at the names tattooed on his fists.

Daddy was going to make this motherfucker *beg*.

*Stephanie Scissom hails from Tennessee, where she lives with her two children, inspects tires by night and plots murder by day. She has four full-length romantic suspense titles and is published in both flash and short story anthologies. Her story, Dandelions, garnered her a Sweek Star recognization and placed first in the international short story competition. Her current project and obsession is an apocalyptic trilogy starring Lucifer, his insane wife, and his deadly, power-hungry siblings*
*Facebook: Stephanie Scissom, Author*
*Twitter: @chell22_7*

# No Paradise
## by Sam M. Phillips

Water is pouring in beneath the doors and through the air vents. Everyone is panicking but I am tranquil. I heard the explosions and knew there was no escape.

People try the doors, but they don't budge. We are trapped, and I'm resigned to fate.

The water level rises, the room filled with screams and thrashing bodies. The water covers my head. I am not worried, soon my reward will come.

As I die, I see an angel staring accusingly at me.

"You did this."

"Yes."

"There will be no paradise for you, no virgins."

And suddenly, I fear death.

*Sam M. Phillips is the co-founder of Zombie Pirate Publishing, producing short story anthologies and helping emerging writers. His own work has appeared in dozens of anthologies and magazines such as Full Moon Slaughter 2, 13 Bites Volumes IV and V, Rejected for Content 6, and Dastaan World Magazine. He lives in the green valleys of northern New South Wales, Australia, and enjoys reading, walking, and playing drums in the death metal band Decryptus.*
*Website: zombiepiratepublishing.com*
*Blog: bigconfusingwords.wordpress.com*

# Pipedreams
## by Shelly Jarvis

Aliessa unfurls her glossy blue-black wings. I watch them stretch behind her—eight, no, ten feet. The feathers aren't soft like a bird's wings, but jagged, sharp, like metal.

Despite her keen senses, she hasn't noticed me. Maybe the techies have finally created an angel-blocking device that works. *Pipedreams*, I think, knowing eventually she'll catch and kill me. These devices never work.

I take aim. I won't get another shot. I ease my finger onto the trigger. *Inhale. Exhale. Release.*

The bullet bounces off her wings. She turns to meet my gaze, a smirk on her lips before she charges.

*Shelly Jarvis is a speculative fiction author from West Virginia, US. She found a life-long love of sci-fi and fantasy in the 3rd grade when she found Madeleine L'Engle's "A Wrinkle in Time." Shelly is an avid reader, a Whovian, the ideal viewer of dog rescue videos, and undoubtedly Ravenclaw. She currently has two YA sci-fi books available for purchase on Amazon.*
*Website: www.ShellyJarvis.com*

# The Last Life
## by David Bowmore

The Guardian of The Dead sent Clay, his trusted deputy, into the world.

Clay's task was to ensure the delivery of the last life.

In a world fraught with disease and darkness, he found her by a glistening stream.

With an innocent smile, she offered him plump fruit from the last surviving tree.

He accepted the offering before carrying out his master's wish, for he was an obedient servant.

Then, weeping for lost beauty, he destroyed his scythe before sprinkling one of his crushed ribs over her remains.

Clay waited for forty days and forty nights.

The magic didn't work.

*David Bowmore has lived here, there and everywhere, but now lives in Yorkshire with his wonderful wife and a small white poodle. He has worn many hats in his time; head chef, teacher and landscape gardener. His first collection of short stories 'The Magic of Deben Market' is available from Clarendon House.*
*Website: davidbowmore.co.uk*
*Facebook: davidbowmoreauthor*

# Game of Souls
## by Crystal L. Kirkham

Everyday, they met for tea; Gabriel and Ifrit, good friends despite playing for opposing teams.

"Today I tempted a man to sin."

"Did you really?" Gabriel said with a grin. "I could have sworn from that darker path he strayed, when he heard me call his name."

"You don't need to rub it in." Ifrit rolled his eyes. "Either way, it's all a game."

"And this time I won his soul." Gabriel held out his hand. "Pay up, old friend."

Ifrit tossed the gold coin into his open palm. "You may have won this time, but the next one's mine."

*Crystal L. Kirkham resides in a small hamlet west of Red Deer, Alberta. She's an avid outdoors person, unrepentant coffee addict, part-time foodie, servant to a wonderful feline, and companion to two delightfully hilarious canines. She will neither confirm nor deny the rumours regarding the heart in a jar on her desk and the bottle of reader's tears right next to it. Her paranormal urban fantasy series, Saints and Sinners, is available on Amazon and her YA Fantasy, Feathers and Fae will be released October 11, 2019, from Kyanite Publishing.*
*Website: www.crystallkirkham.com*

# Feathers and Flesh
## by Jo Seysener

"It's agreed, then?"

"I stand by my word."

"Not sure I trust that. Sign it. With your best feather."

"*You* don't trust *me?*"

"I've said as much, 'aven't I? I like this black one, right 'ere."

The demon flinched as the creature filched his most prized feather.

"That stung."

The humped angel signed the contract while he rubbed the aching flesh.

*I'd like to pluck you.*

"Too many liberties."

"Wait 'til we take souls." Stone swirled, melted beneath their feet.

"The right ones."

"But of course."

"Pass the feather."

"Why?"

"I'll sign for my soul with my own bloody feather."

*Jo Seysener* is a mum of three crazies, a scatter of chickens, a decrepit kelpie and a rambunctious GSD. She lives with her husband near Brisbane, Australia. When she is not exposing her kids to cult story books from her childhood, she can be found in the kitchen experimenting with new flavours and pairings. She adores alpacas.

*Facebook: joseysener*
*Website: www.joseysener.com*

# Locker
## by Phil Dyer

Here come the angels again, lads! Look at that lovely light. Bet she makes a thousand fathoms this time.

Which one of you are they so keen for, eh? Knew we had a god-fearing man among us.

Ha! Back up she goes. What's wrong, love, too dark down here? Back to the shallows, you firefly.

Oho, you devils, I haven't forgotten. Come up to grab us, will you? Crawl, you maggots, crawl! The weight of the Atlantic rest upon you, flat as pancakes, red as starfish all.

Here we sank and here we stay. Come claim us if you can.

*Phil Dyer does medical research in Liverpool and writes spec fic on the side. His stories have appeared in Unfit Magazine, 101 Words and The Drabble. He retweets animal videos.*
*Twitter: @ez_ozel*

# God
## by Preveena Sivakumar

I woke up here. A cave, I thought, but it was wet, I felt a scorching heat but no sun or light. Only darkness.

"Welcome, mortal!" An eerie voice echoed.

*Who are you?* I thought to myself; I seemed to have lost my speech.

"All mortals know me," It said.

*Is this heaven?* I was confused.

"No," It answered.

I don't understand; I prayed, I committed no sin. I was—am—a good man. *Why am I not in Heaven?*

Silence followed. I waited for an answer. I know he heard my thoughts.

"Foolish mortal," It said finally.

*Where is God?*

"I am God."

*Preveena Sivakumar is a Malaysian horror author who has published an anthology, 'Scared: A Malaysian Horror Anthology'. As a horror lover, she meddles with all thing horror even though being easily scared herself. She also has a Youtube channel which narrated all thing scary in Asia: TimeTravelling Storyteller.*

# Invite
## by Umair Mirxa

Ishmael took a deep breath and opened the door. He smiled at his guest and asked him inside.

"I must say," said the visitor. "I'm not used to entering a home with an invite, much less a warm smile. To what do I owe the pleasure?"

"I would like to die, please."

"Aren't you full of surprises? Well, if you have made your choice."

"What do I have to do?"

"Simply take my hand."

It had never happened before—a human choosing him willingly, and the Angel of Death suspected it never would again as he led Ishmael away.

*Umair Mirxa lives in Karachi, Pakistan. His first published story, 'Awareness', appeared on Spillwords Press. He has also had stories accepted for anthologies from Zombie Pirate Publishing, Blood Song Books, Fantasia Divinity Magazine and Publishing, and Iron Faerie Publishing. He is a massive J.R.R. Tolkien fan, and loves everything to do with fantasy and mythology. He enjoys football, history, music, movies, TV shows, and comic books, and wishes with all his heart that dragons were real.*
*Website: www.umairmirxa.com*
*Facebook: UMirxa12*

# Kenji and the Spirit Warrior
## by J.D. Bell

Tears poured down Kenji's cheeks. The barbaric Mirimoto clan had murdered his father and uncle. He cursed himself for being so weak. The clan members laughed at his feeble attempts to stop the killings.

As the sun set, a ghostly figure appeared before him. "Do not be afraid little one. I am a Tengu, a spirit of great warriors past. My master sent me to share mastery of swordsmanship with you. You will have justice."

At the full moon, the leader of the clan received a messenger bearing a large crate. Inside were the heads of his twelve best swordsmen.

*J.D. Bell is an award-winning, internationally published, author of flash fiction and short stories. He recently retired from the world of writing advertising copy and is now enjoying the universe of creative fiction.*
*Facebook: jim.writes.stories*
*Twitter: @JimBell58*

# Judgement
## by R.J. Hunt

The clouds parted, and High-Angel Gabriel stepped down. As his foot touched the earth, he became human; wings folding away, shimmering gold skin dulling to tanned flesh.

"I didn't think you'd come," said Lucifer, brushing a finger against his lip. In the presence of a high angel, his horns revealed themselves, along with his burnt wing stumps.

"He did not want me to," admitted Gabriel.

"So…?" Lucifer asked with a smile. "You think I should be stopped?"

Gabriel paused, his eyes lingering on the human war machines and dead bodies, scattered all around.

"I think we can all do better."

*R.J. Hunt is a Civil Engineer from Nottingham who loves creating worlds and writing stories in his spare time. Whilst he has a roughly infinite supply of half-finished stories, he's currently working on the second draft of his debut novel, 'The Final Carnivore' - a story about horrible people being granted immortality and mind-control powers, causing misfits with hidden abilities of their own to rise in an effort stop them.*
*Twitter: @RJHuntWrites*
*Reddit: RJHuntWrites*

# The Warning
## by R.G. Halstead

After Mrs. Cooper had gone shopping. Her husband was looking after little Tommy Nash while his parents attended a funeral. Little boys shouldn't attend funerals. Her husband thought differently. He just wanted to write short stories. Not baby-sit.

The old man had warned her that he didn't like kids. But she had talked him into baby-sitting Tommy.

The curious little snot; full of questions.

"What's your story about, Mr. Cooper?" Tommy asked.

"A demon and an angel have a baby."

"Wow. What does it look like?"

"Like me. I was...am...that baby."

Tommy dropped dead from shock.

"I warned her."

*R.G. Halstead, a 63-year-old, takes to writing late in his life. Influences? Those old Alfred Hitchcock Mystery Magazines from the late 1950s and the 1960s with the great twisty endings. Love them.*

# A Flock of Angels
## by Brian Rosenberger

After the robbery.

Shot in the leg. Could be worse. Could be James.

I met James at a brothel. We raised Hell ever since. His brain exploded on our getaway.

Goddamn Marshall had great aim, drunk or not. I had the money bags and rode on.

James wasn't the only one to catch lead. My horse died miles out of town.

The bullet is a problem. Reluctantly, I drop the money bags. Too much of a burden.

Burning sun. Canteen empty.

Angels circle. A flock of them.

They look like feathered morticians. Black and hungry.

Not angels after all.

Vultures.

*Brian Rosenberger lives in a cellar in Marietta, GA (USA) and writes by the light of captured fireflies. He is the author of As the Worms Turns and three poetry collections. He is also a featured contributor to the Pro-Wrestling literary collection, Three-Way Dance, available from Gimmick Press.*
*Facebook: HeWhoSuffers*

# Pursuit
## by G. Allen Wilbanks

The demon launched itself into the air on leathery wings and, the moment it left the ground, the angel was in pursuit. The hellspawn was quick, but the feathered wings of the chasing angel beat fiercely, closing the distance between the two.

Realising it could not escape by speed alone, the demon furled its wings and let gravity pull it back to earth. It had one more gambit to try before accepting the inevitable defeat.

"Time out," it cried, extending taloned hands defensively.

"There is no time out," the angel laughed, pressing a finger to the demon's shoulder. "You're it."

*G. Allen Wilbanks is a member of the Horror Writers Association (HWA) and has published over 50 short stories in various magazines and on-line venues. He is the author of two short story collections, and the novel, When Darkness Comes.*
*Website: www.gallenwilbanks.com*
*Blog: DeepDarkThoughts.com*

# A Wolf's Confession
## by Wendy Roberts

Kristen stands at the bottom of the stairs, staring at the cross on the wooden doors. She wants to confess her sins and do however many Hail Marys it would take to wash the blood from her hands. It's what she would have done in her old life. It's how her father would have handled this situation where she's a sheep in wolf's clothing.

"Another kill's been reported. Are we off to feed tonight?"

Her human side gags at the thought of hunting a fellow murderer and realises she'll have to make her confessions to God while revenging his innocent.

*Writing short stories and novels started as a past time for* **Wendy Roberts** *and has now become a fully-fledged passion. She posts short stories on her website and can be found most days on twitter.*
*Website: flippinscribbler.wordpress.com*
*Twitter: @_WARoberts*

# Haste Makes Waste
## by John H. Dromey

In the time of King Minos, a Cretan merchant needed to communicate with someone on a nearby island.

"Ships are too slow. I entrusted my missive to a winged messenger."

"Hermes?"

"No, a mortal human. Can't remember his name."

"Very few of them fly. Daedalus?"

"No, the other one."

"Icarus might be an unfortunate choice."

"Why?"

"Let's just say he's no angel. His hubris could inspire him to soar to heavenly heights and thereby draw dangerously close to the sun."

The merchant flinched. "Something hot just hit my cheek." He touched the spot with his finger. "I think it's wax."

*John H. Dromey was born in northeast Missouri, USA. He enjoys reading—mysteries in particular—and writing in a variety of genres. He's had short fiction published in Alfred Hitchcock's Mystery Magazine, Martian Magazine, Stupefying Stories Showcase, Thriller Magazine, Unfit Magazine, and elsewhere, as well as in a number of anthologies, including Chilling Horror Short Stories (Flame Tree Publishing, 2015).*

# Heralds of Light and Darkness
## by Pamela Jeffs

Water and phosphorescence drips off the stone walls of the cave. The dark angel, Herald of the Night, leans against the far wall. He smiles at me, trapped as I am in his cage. "Without you, the sun will never rise again," he says. "The world will fall to chaos."

I frown. "Release me."

"No."

I rise. My wings brush the bottom of my prison; their feathered tips come away stained.

"Darkness shall not reign." As Herald of the Light, I lift my voice in song. The sun cannot hear me, but the phosphorescence answers, rising to my luminous call.

*Pamela Jeffs* *is a speculative fiction author living in Queensland, Australia with her husband and two daughters. She is a member of the Queensland Writers' Centre and has had numerous short fiction pieces published in recent national and international anthologies. In 2017 and again in 2018, Pamela was nominated for an Australian Aurealis Award in the category of 'Best Science Fiction Short Story'. Her debut collection titled 'Red Hour and Other Strange Tales' was released in March 2018.*
*Website: www.pamelajeffs.com*
*Facebook: pamelajeffsauthor*

# Carving
## by Vonnie Winslow Crist

Everyday as Clem looked after the ranch's horses, he heard angels in the trees. Each evening, he'd select a piece of wood he'd collected earlier, hold it in his hand, and listen for wings. Then, Clem would pull out a penknife, begin carving, and free the trapped angel.

"Ain't you tired of whittling, angels?" asked another stable hand.

"Never," answered Clem.

"Well, I'm tired of seeing them." The man grabbed some angels, tossed them into their campfire.

The fire flared, an angel stepped out and incinerated the stable hand. She turned to Clem, said, "Keep carving,"

He nodded, resumed whittling.

*Vonnie Winslow Crist is author of The Enchanted Dagger, Owl Light, The Greener Forest, Murder on Marawa Prime, and other award-winning books. Her fiction is included in "Amazing Stories," "Cast of Wonders," "Outposts of Beyond," Killing It Softly 2, Defending the Future - Dogs of War, Midnight Masquerade, Chaos of Hard Clay, and elsewhere. A cloverhand who has found so many four-leafed clovers she keeps them in jars, Vonnie strives to celebrate the power of myth in her writing.*
*Website: www.vonniewinslowcrist.com*

# Enveloped by Darkness
by Rowanne S. Carberry

"The bastard fired me! Then sent a video of him fucking my wife."

Pacing the room, he ignores the voices of the angel and devil on his shoulders, brought to life from the tattoos on his arms.

The demon smirks, whispering in his ears.

"Kill him." The whispers grow louder. "Make him pay." Darkness begins to envelop his thoughts.

"Let's go out," the angel says, "think things through."

The man nods and the angel smiles.

A flex of his left arm, she's frozen as a tattoo, eyes wide.

He chooses a knife and walks outside, the demon riding his shoulder.

*Rowanne S. Carberry was born in England in 1990, where she stills lives now with her cat Wolverine. Rowanne has always loved writing, and her first poem was published at the age of 15, but her ambition has always been to help people. Rowanne studied at the University of Sunderland where she completed combined honours of Psychology with Drama. Rowanne writes to offer others an escape. Although Rowanne writes in varied genres each story or poem she writes will often have a darkness to it, which helped coin her brand, Poisoned Quill Writing – Wicked words from a poisoned quill.*
*Facebook: PoisonedQuillWriting*
*Instagram: @poisoned_quill_writing*

# Aftermath
## by Beth W. Patterson

In the Dark Ages, they called you a fallen angel. Now they call you PTSD.

You were created to protect us, but you were obsessed. Oh, Morning Star, Lucifer, must you make everything so shockingly bright with this hypervigilance?

The boss didn't like your ambition, and you were fired. So, you got a job with the rival security company. And now that the war in Heaven had ceased, Hell follows me every waking moment, as if keeping me close to you is the only way to shield me. No drug erases your legacy.

PTSD stands for Put That Sword Down.

*Beth W. Patterson was a full-time musician for over two decades before diving into the world of writing, a process she describes as "fleeing the circus to join the zoo". She is the author of the books Mongrels and Misfits, and The Wild Harmonic, and a contributing writer to twenty anthologies. Patterson has performed in eighteen countries, expanding her perspective as she goes. Her playing appears on over a hundred and sixty albums, soundtracks, videos, commercials, and voice-overs (including seven solo albums of her own). She lives in New Orleans, Louisiana with her husband Josh Paxton, jazz pianist extraordinaire.*
*Website: www.bethpattersonmusic.com*
*Facebook: bethodist*

# Two for One
## by Alexander Pyles

"Please, put the gun down." Gabby always wanted the best for me.

"No, take it," Lucas hissed. "You need it."

The pair stood on my shoulders. Gabby's wings always tickled, while Lucas' feet burned. "Why?"

"There are bad people. Take care of yourself, kid." His saccharine voice melting into my ear, like candy on the tongue

"You don't need it or this snake." The seraph straightened her robe.

"And I'm the liar?" Lucas' tail snapped.

Before either could tussle, I caught both their wings in one hand and levelled the gun with the other. All it took was one pull.

*Alexander Pyles resides in IL with his wife and children. He holds an MA in Philosophy and an MFA in Writing Popular Fiction. His short story chapbook titled, "Milo (01001101 01101001 01101100 01101111)," from Radix Media, is due out fall 2019. His other short fiction has appeared on 101fiction.org, River and South Review, and other venues. Website: www.pylesofbooks.com Twitter: @Pylesofbooks*

# I'm So Tired
## by Stephen Herczeg

Lord Lucifer unleashed the hordes of hell. We met them on the Earthly plane.

Our mission; stop the forces of evil and protect the sons and daughters of Adam.

My flaming sword sung as I slashed the demons that surrounded me. The ground was awash with their blood. I thought the carnage would never end.

The Morningstar rose from the putrid depths of the abyss.

The Archangels led us against him. Many fell, but we finally succeeded and sent Satan back to the netherworld.

My sword is notched and dull and I'm so tired. I could sleep for a century.

*Stephen Herczeg is an IT Geek based in Canberra Australia. He has been writing for over twenty years and has completed a couple of dodgy novels, sixteen feature length screenplays and numerous short stories and scripts. His horror work has featured in Sproutlings, Hells Bells, Below the Stairs, Trickster's Treats #1 and #2, Shades of Santa, Behind the Mask, Beyond the Infinite; The Body Horror Book, Anemone Enemy, Petrified Punks and Beginnings. He has also had numerous Sherlock Holmes stories published through the Belanger Books - Sherlock Holmes anthologies.*

# 72 Hours for Observations
## by Raven Corinn Carluk

Dr. Goldberg skimmed the file before him as the restrained man waited. "You call yourself Abaddon." This was the eighth man saying he was an angel this week.

"It's what the Almighty gave me."

"How long have you believed yourself to be an angel?"

"Since the Word."

Dr. Goldberg sighed, writing orders for heavy doses of Thorazine.

"Won't work on me."

He arched his brow. "Pardon?"

The man called Abaddon smiled, feral, wicked. "Unlike my former brothers that you've confined already, I'm Fallen. I won't hesitate to lift my sword against humans." He broke free of his restraints and rose.

*Raven Corinn Carluk is an indie author of dark fantasy and paranormal romance.*
*Website: RavenCorinnCarluk.Blogspot.Com*

# The Devil's Consort
by Martin Eastland

She lay there on the vast table, her arms and legs manacled, the officiators performing the rites as she looked on, her eyes wide in terror. The blood from the innocent child they had sacrificed a bare moment earlier was being held aloft in deference to the Baphomet effigy behind her.

The chanting began, sending chills to the depths of her soul.

*Am I crazy, or is the room getting colder?* she thought. The hooded, emblemed figures with their heads up, their hands stretched out, their fingers livid, joined as one in their cacophony of evil. Darkness enveloped her, finally.

*Born in Glasgow, Scotland, **Martin Eastland** began his writing career at the age of 12, his only outlet allowing him to escape a less than harmonious childhood. Almost 30 years later, he has gone from strength to strength as a writer, expanding into new areas, but remaining loyal to his preferred genres of horror, and the suspense-thriller. He enjoys mainly short stories and flash fiction as he views it as being beneficial for his future development as an author. He is happily married with four children, and lives with his wife in Shropshire, England.*
*Facebook: Martin-Eastland-245154596385827*

# Man Who Cannot Sleep
by Rickey Rivers Jr.

He sat in the kitchen, his head in his hands.

Soon his daughter stood in the doorway. "Daddy, I'm tired."

Lazily he stood and walked her back to her room. "Goodnight dear," he said, and kissed her sizzling forehead.

He went back to the kitchen and sat, head in his hands.

Soon his daughter stood in the doorway. "Daddy, I'm tired."

Again, he walked her back to her room and kissed her blistering forehead. "Goodnight dear," he said. He returned to the kitchen.

"Please," he said to the watcher, "let me sleep."

But soon his daughter stood in the doorway.

*Rickey Rivers Jr. was born and raised in Alabama. He is a writer and cancer survivor. He likes a lot of stuff. You don't care about the details. He has been previously published in Fabula Argentea, ARTPOST magazine, the anthology Chronos, Enchanted Conversations Magazine, (among other publications).*
*Twitter: @storiesyoumight*

# Angel on My Shoulder
## by J. Farrington

I think the Angel on my shoulder has gone rogue.

I know what that sounds like, hear me out.

When I was young, and faced with a moral dilemma, the angel and demon on opposing shoulders would state their case for what they thought I should do. Lately, the Demon hasn't been showing up, you'd think that wouldn't be a problem.

You're wrong.

The angel thinks that, to be fair, he must fight the argument for both sides, but I think he's lost his way.

He's started to steer me down the darkened path.

And I think I like it.

*J. Farrington is an aspiring author from the West Midlands, UK. His genre of choice is horror; whether that be psychological, suspense, supernatural or straight up weird, he'll give it a shot! He has loved writing from a young age but has only publicly been spreading his darker thoughts and sinister imagination via social platforms since 2018. If you would like to view his previous work, or merely lurk in the shadows...watching, you can keep up to date with future projects by spirit board or alternatively, the following;*
*Twitter: @SurvivorTrench*
*Reddit: TrenchChronicles*

# Protector
## by Raven Corinn Carluk

Turmael lashed out with his sword. Lightning crackled along the blade, arcing against inky carapace as the angel sliced through demon flesh. The being shrieked before collapsing in a pile of mush.

One down, three dozen left.

Turmael spun and charged the next demon. He plunged it into the heart of his target. The battle would end soon.

A woman tugged on his wing, pulling his attention from the fight. "Are you my guardian angel?" Blood stained her face, and a fire raged nearby. She wept, a dead child beside her.

Turmael sneered. "Of course not." He returned to battle.

*Raven Corinn Carluk is an indie author of dark fantasy and paranormal romance.*
*Website: RavenCorinnCarluk.Blogspot.Com*

# The Fallen
## by Michael Crow

Azazel's black feathered, four-winged form loomed over Michael in stark contrast to the purity of his glowing white.

"Ah! The great Archangel Michael. Your number is punched, friend."

"Azazel, I'm just a vessel of my Lord, His bringer of light. My Father who will come is much greater than I." Michael growled struggling against the restraints that held him fast to the altar.

"Enough!" Azazel hefted the immense onyx sword overhead. "You first, then your Father and then the rest of his people!"

A swift stroke, a burst of light, and a sonic boom. Michael was no more.

"Bring Gabriel next."

*Michael Crow spends his sparse free time writing about sports, as well as working on his own fiction. Michael is the owner of Real Dead Review, a blog devoted to dark fiction. Michael's non-fiction works have appeared on USA Today, Fansided Network, The Guillotine, and Intermat. Michael makes his home with his wife, daughter and two cats in Central Minnesota.*

# His Love
## by David Bowmore

God was not pleased.

He could read the hearts of men, but angels were a mystery.

Why did this angel persist in whining?

"De-wing him and send him down," he ordered the Seraphim.

* * *

Falling like a fiery stone, the angel crashed into the Earth with enough force to leave a crater.

Someone held a pitcher to his lips.

"Come, there is a place where all the Lord's exiles can live in peace without fear of reprisal for refusing His selfish demands."

"But He loves all His creations."

"This isn't love," Lucifer said, rubbing healing balm onto the burnt flesh.

*David Bowmore has lived here, there and everywhere, but now lives in Yorkshire with his wonderful wife and a small white poodle. He has worn many hats in his time; head chef, teacher and landscape gardener. His first collection of short stories 'The Magic of Deben Market' is available from Clarendon House.*
*Website: davidbowmore.co.uk*
*Facebook: davidbowmoreauthor*

# Duty
## by Joel R. Hunt

William peered into the corner of the tavern where an old sea captain sat shrouded in darkness. He approached with a whisper.

"They say you've seen an angel."

"Aye," replied the captain, "they say that."

Coins were placed on the table.

"Tell me everything."

"What I saw can't be told. There ain't the words for it. So beautiful, she was, like nothing I ever dreamed. I'd have sailed my ship right into the rocks beneath her if my crew had let me."

"What did they do?"

The captain leant forwards. Light fell into empty eye sockets.

"What they had to."

*Joel R. Hunt is a writer from the UK who dabbles in the darker aspects of life, particularly through horror, science fiction and the supernatural. He has been published here and there (though likely nowhere you've heard of) and hopes to have released his first anthology of short stories later this year.*
*Twitter: @JoelRHunt1*
*Reddit: JRHEvilInc*

# Eternal Battle
## by Sinister Sweetheart

Soldiers who throw themselves on grenades to save their comrades. Teachers who shield children from classroom shooters. Pilots who steer their failing planes towards water; they all know they will die so that others may live.

The saviours of hope; these are angels.

Terrorists, the fatally driven, zealots of pain and destruction. The owners of vans transporting missing children. Those taking the lives of parents, children and spouses, just to add to their bank accounts.

The crushers of dreams; these are Demons.

Angels and demons locked in an eternal battle. The fate of the world rests on their next move.

*Since **Sinister Sweetheart** made her first post to a popular Internet forum, she's taken the horror community by storm. Her ability to create, terrify, and drive home her stories is insurmountable. Sinister Sweetheart's published works can be found in multiple anthologies for all to read, but be forewarned, if you do... you may want to call your therapist after, her stories are terrifying, disturbing and devilishly unsettling. She is not only a fright visually, but also has a creepy tentacle in horror podcasting as well. Sinister Sweetheart writes, voice acts and is the media director of the Scarecrow Tales podcast.*
*Website: Sinistersweetheart.wixsite.com/sinistersweetheart*
*Facebook: NMBrownStories*

# Hatred
## by Umair Mirxa

Halfnìr leaned against the charred tree, glad for a moment's respite. They had battled, Kjartan and him, for hours. Maybe days. He could no longer tell.

The axe whistled as it swung in the rain. He ducked, slashed Kjartan's thigh, and pivoted away.

"Brother, stop," he said. "I beg of you. Do not let your hatred be—"

"My hatred?" snarled Kjartan, burying the dagger deeper into Halfnìr's throat. "How easily you angels forget and forgive. Demon memories aren't quite as fickle, brother. The humans will know despair. I will never forgive."

He dropped the dead angel and walked away.

*Umair Mirxa lives in Karachi, Pakistan. His first published story, 'Awareness', appeared on Spillwords Press. He has also had stories accepted for anthologies from Zombie Pirate Publishing, Blood Song Books, Fantasia Divinity Magazine and Publishing, and Iron Faerie Publishing. He is a massive J.R.R. Tolkien fan, and loves everything to do with fantasy and mythology. He enjoys football, history, music, movies, TV shows, and comic books, and wishes with all his heart that dragons were real.*
*Website: www.umairmirxa.com*
*Facebook: UMirxa12*

# The Sacrifice
## by Eddie D. Moore

Arron gasped dumbfounded at the beauty and strength of the creature before him.

The angel folded massive wings and met Arron's eyes. "Why have you called me?"

Arron swallowed the lump in his throat. "My mother is dying in the room above us. I would like her to be healed."

The angel closed his eyes a moment and then said, "It's done."

"Wow, I wonder why you always hear about people conjuring demons but never angels?"

The angel laughed. "That's simple. A demon is summoned by sacrificing someone else's life. An angel is summoned at the expense of your own."

*Eddie D. Moore travels extensively for work, and he spends much of that time listening to audio books. The rest of the time is spent dreaming of stories to write and he spends the weekends writing them. His stories have been published by Jouth Webzine, Kzine, Alien Dimensions, Theme of Absence, Devolution Z, and Fantasia Divinity Magazine.*
*Website: eddiedmoore.wordpress.com*

# The Baroque Angel
## by John K. Webb

"Mr. Misaki, forgive the intrusion," I say, walking into the office.

The aging meat of this Japanese tech baron looks up from his desk and squints.

"Don't think I know you," he says.

"Oh, sure you do." I sit. "We've known each other for centuries."

"How did you get in here?"

With a whisper of song, I manifest the burning broadsword. Smoke billows.

"You've been away far too long."

Misaki's face tightens with panic.

"Don't…don't—!" The meat stutters.

"Everyone's waiting, my Lord."

I bring the blade down, so ending His fevered dream of man on wings of flame.

*John K. Webb enjoys fantasy, science fiction, and wants everyone to know that he's doing his best. He resides in Richmond, Virginia, where he's currently studying English and scribbling down whatever comes to mind.*

# Kids Today Are Not Angels
## by R.G. Halstead

Sitting in the city park, the old man could only think that kids today were crazed demons with foul mouths. Well, all those drugs and booze were going to cause their lives to come crashing down on them.

The beautiful statue of the angel in the middle of the water fountain gave him hope, though.

God would take care of the destructive demon gangs running wild in the park.

The puzzled old man saw them pushing at the base of the statue. He heard a sound. *What the—*

He felt the pain of the concrete angel crushing him to death.

*R.G. Halstead, a 63-year-old, takes to writing late in his life. Influences? Those old Alfred Hitchcock Mystery Magazines from the late 1950s and the 1960s with the great twisty endings. Love them.*

# Where Other Angels Fear to Tread
## by John H. Dromey

"Is it true you collided with a flock of Canadian geese?"

"That wasn't entirely my fault, Boss. Their migration was unseasonable because of climate change. They should have honked."

"Another thing, Ike. With your head in the clouds, you need to watch your step. I hear you tumbled through a hole in the ozone layer and landed on an outdoor jumble sale table covered with devil's food cakes. Then you licked the icing off your feathers with a happy expression on your face. Fair warning. Straighten up and fly right, or I'll have to reclassify you as a fallen angel."

*John H. Dromey was born in northeast Missouri, USA. He enjoys reading—mysteries in particular—and writing in a variety of genres. He's had short fiction published in Alfred Hitchcock's Mystery Magazine, Martian Magazine, Stupefying Stories Showcase, Thriller Magazine, Unfit Magazine, and elsewhere, as well as in a number of anthologies, including Chilling Horror Short Stories (Flame Tree Publishing, 2015).*

# Little Daniel
## by Ximena Escobar

Leila buttered the bread. "No more," she'd told him, "because it's not good for you."

His little heart in his little chest. His little veins, his little arms. How can someone so little stretch your heart to infinity; your heart extended like land in the eternal warm sunset of his existence. Your every purpose just to love him; nothing more, nothing less.

She cleaned the knife.

"Daniel?"

Her heart pounded until now. When she lies awake haunted by the moment when she knew, thank the angels, he'd just fallen in the pond. Thank the length of a dollop of butter.

*Ximena Escobar is an emerging author of literary fiction and poetry. Originally from Chile, she is the author of a translation into Spanish of the Broadway Musical "The Wizard of Oz", and of an original adaptation of the same, "Navidad en Oz". Clarendon House Publications published her first short story in the UK, "The Persistence of Memory", and Literally Stories her first online publication with "The Green Light". She has since had several acceptances from other publishers and is working very hard exploring new exciting avenues in her writing.*
*She lives in Nottingham with her family.*
*Facebook: Ximenautora*

# Frozen Dream
## by Dawn DeBraal

The Book of Job tells us angels oversaw the creation and still watch over us.

At -30°C, Christina knew she should have stayed home. Now she was in the ditch. She prayed someone would find her before she froze to death. Help came in the form of a tow truck. The gentleman tapped on her window, waking her from sleep. He pulled her car out of the snow, onto the road.

"Let me pay you." Gratefully, Christina reached for her purse, handing cash out of the car window. The man and the tow truck were gone. Had she dreamed this?

*Dawn DeBraal lives in rural Wisconsin with her husband, two rat terriers, and a cat. She successfully raised two children (meaning they didn't return to the nest!) After many years serving the government at the Federal and County level, she recently retired. Having extra time on her hands she started to write after a paralyzed vocal cord took her ability to speak for two months. Not finding her voice, she discovered that her love of telling a good story could be written. Her works have been published in Palm-Sized Press, Spillwords, Mercurial Stories, Potato Soup Journal, and Blood Song Books.*

# The Angel of Death
## by Zoey Xolton

With wings as black as the Abyss, Samael stood beside the Throne, defying all earthly means of measure. Studded with glaring eyes from crown to heel, he was terrifying to behold. Metatron laid a hand upon Moses' quaking shoulder to calm him. "Fear not," he said. "Samael is the Reaper, claimer of the souls of men. He is neither good, nor evil. He goes now to reap the soul of Job the Pious."

Moses wept with relief and prayed that he might never fall into the hands of such an angel.

"All must meet him, one day," said Metatron gravely.

*Zoey Xolton is an Australian Speculative Fiction writer, primarily of Dark Fantasy, Paranormal Romance and Horror. She is also a proud mother of two and is married to her soul mate. Outside of her family, writing is her greatest passion. She is especially fond of short fiction and is working on releasing her own themed collections in future.*
*Website: www.zoeyxolton.com*

# Devil Child
## by R.G. Halstead

After trying for years to make a deal with Satan, the young couple had finally gotten pregnant. But only after desperately turning to God for help.

When the Smiths came home from the hospital months later, there was an addition to their family; little Angel Maria Smith. The cutest little girl in the world.

When they pulled the car into the driveway, they were shocked to see a message spray painted on their garage door. And on their house's windows.

*Nice Try.*

Startled more than her husband, the mother hugged her little Angel. She was cold. Lifeless.

Dead.

*Nice try.*

*R.G. Halstead, a 63-year-old, takes to writing late in his life. Influences? Those old Alfred Hitchcock Mystery Magazines from the late 1950s and the 1960s with the great twisty endings. Love them.*

# Opposites Attract
## by Nerisha Kemraj

Greta knew he was different by the way she was drawn to him. So, on his eighteenth birthday when he begged to be alone, she followed him into the woods anyway. He needed support, like she did. She had her mom when she changed. He had nobody.

She watched, secretly. His harrowing screams pierced the forest as two wings tore through his back—breaking through flesh. He silenced at the sound of a snapping twig—eyes frozen in terror.

"Relax." She lifted hair from her forehead, exposing two red stubs where horns were shaved off. "I changed, too."

*Multi-genre (short-fiction) author, and poet, **Nerisha Kemraj**, resides in South Africa with her husband and two, mischievous daughters. She has work traditionally published/accepted in 30 publications, thus far, both print and online. She holds a BA in Communication Science from UNISA and is currently busy with a Post-Graduate Certificate in Education.*
*Facebook: Nerishakemrajwriter*

# A Storm Over Constantinople
## by Aiki Flinthart

The crackle and zip of lightning curls about me, teasing. Sharp winds carry the warm scent of ozone. High on the palace tower, I call on Barachiel. She rides a lightning bolt to my side. Her arms slide about me, her glowing face lifts for my kiss.

"Emperor Justinian." Her voice is the soft roll of distant thunder. Her lips taste of rain.

"You appointed a guardian angel for Justin, my nephew?"

Irritation flickers through her grey eyes. "He'll be Emperor, soon."

"I'm not ready."

"Not your choice." She smiles, cool.

My dagger slides into her heart. "Yes, it is."

*Aiki Flinthart has had short stories shortlisted in the Aurealis awards and top-8 listed in the USA Writers of the Future competition, as well as published in various anthologies and e-mags. She has 11 published spec fic novels and has edited 2 short story anthologies. She regularly gives workshops on writing fight scenes at conventions. Lives in Brisbane. Does martial arts, archery, knife throwing and lute-playing.*
*Website: www.aikiflinthart.com*

# Fallen Angel
## by Destiny Eve Pifer

Falling, falling through the clouds, through the darkness. Falling to the hard, green grass below.

Waking up, Molly had no idea what had happened except that she had given in to temptation; given in to the whispers of a more promising existence. Now here she lay upon the moist green earth.

Her white dress clung to her hourglass figure and the white wings she once had were now just a dark grey ash.

"What have I done?" she whispered to herself. She had given up an eternity of bliss to live among the wicked.

"Welcome to Hell!" said the devil.

*Destiny Eve Pifer is a published author whose work has appeared in numerous anthologies and magazines. Her stories have been featured in FATE Magazine, True Confessions, Spotlight on Recovery and Country Magazine. A lover of all things supernatural and spooky she resides in Punxsutawney, Pennsylvania with her son Dartanyan.*

# Into the Clouds
## by Will Shadbolt

When Abraham died and became an angel, he discovered hell. It was not a place; no fires, no brimstone. It was the wings.

He had no control over them. At first, as they took him through cloud and storm, he thought they led him to heaven. But no golden gates emerged from the foggy white.

"It ain't coming," said a voice.

Angels, it turned out, were not favoured by God. Their wings were demons latched onto bodies.

"We're in a symbiotic relationship. Whatever you call it," said the wings. "Your legends were right about one thing, though. We're immortal now."

*Will Shadbolt has lived across the world, including in Germany and China. He currently works in NYC. His fiction has appeared in Daily Science Fiction and numerous drabble anthologies.*

# Twinkle, Twinkle, Little Star
by Brian Rosenberger

We thought meteorites at first. They fell from space and impacted Earth. Curiously, no satellite or other tracking system detected them; they were visible only to the naked eye. We called them falling stars.

*Make a wish...*

The big brains investigated the craters. The remains. Feathers.

Craters...more like graves.

The theologians had it right first. Beating the astronomers, the physicists, NASA, the press, etc.

Another war in Heaven was being waged. We were witness to the casualties.

Saint and sinner, believers and blasphemers, atheists, agnostics, and the casual observer. All united in prayer.

That Mankind would survive the aftermath.

*Brian Rosenberger lives in a cellar in Marietta, GA (USA) and writes by the light of captured fireflies. He is the author of As the Worms Turns and three poetry collections. He is also a featured contributor to the Pro-Wrestling literary collection, Three-Way Dance, available from Gimmick Press.*
*Facebook: HeWhoSuffers*

# Fresh Meat
## by Eddie D. Moore

Jason double checked his equipment and prepared to repel into the dark cavern. "The locals say a fallen angel landed here and made this cave."

Kevin cupped a hand by his mouth and shouted, "Fresh meat coming down!" He grinned at his companion and said, "I mean good luck."

Jason descended and vanished from sight. Kevin's radio beeped, and Jason said, "I see the bottom."

Seconds later, a scream echoed in the darkness.

Kevin spoke frantically into his radio. "Jason, can you hear me? Are you okay?"

The radio beeped and a raspy voice said, "I'm fine, come on down."

*Eddie D. Moore travels extensively for work, and he spends much of that time listening to audio books. The rest of the time is spent dreaming of stories to write and he spends the weekends writing them. His stories have been published by Jouth Webzine, Kzine, Alien Dimensions, Theme of Absence, Devolution Z, and Fantasia Divinity Magazine.*
*Website: eddiedmoore.wordpress.com*

# Whatever it Takes
## by Stuart Conover

Daniel swore.

Summoning a demon was dangerous, but an angel was just frustrating.

The sacrifices were the same.

Blood, the possible forfeiture of one's soul.

The rewards were falling short.

"I need one last day with Sam" he cried out.

Devi the Bringer of Light was unmoved.

"I just can't help."

All of the preparation couldn't be for nothing.

"What did I do wrong?" he eked out.

"My friend," the divine being explained, "Sam's soul didn't come to us."

"Perhaps I could help" came a voice from the shadows.

Daniel knew he'd do whatever it took to see Sam again.

*Stuart Conover is a father, husband, rescue dog owner, published author, blogger, journalist, horror enthusiast, comic book geek, science fiction junkie, and IT professional. With all of that to cram in daily, we have no idea if or when he sleeps or how he gets writing done! (We suspect it has to do with having evil clones.) Stuart is a Chicago native and runs the author resource Horror Tree.*

# The Devourer
## by Rowanne S. Carberry

The smell of sulphur permeates the air making it hard to breathe.

Stephen struggles home through the darkness. A million thoughts running through his mind, he doesn't look up from his phone.

Eyes of fire stare from ahead, drool falls from fangs, venom drips from claws.

The demon slithers from the drain. The noise forcing Stephen to look up.

His face drains of colour, paralysed to the spot.

The demon stalks closer. Stephen's adrenalin kicks in, he runs.

A game of chase. The demon runs before pouncing. Claws digging in, it rips out his heart, devouring it with a smile.

***Rowanne S. Carberry*** *was born in England in 1990, where she stills lives now with her cat Wolverine. Rowanne has always loved writing, and her first poem was published at the age of 15, but her ambition has always been to help people. Rowanne studied at the University of Sunderland where she completed combined honours of Psychology with Drama. Rowanne writes to offer others an escape. Although Rowanne writes in varied genres each story or poem she writes will often have a darkness to it, which helped coin her brand, Poisoned Quill Writing – Wicked words from a poisoned quill.*

*Facebook: PoisonedQuillWriting*

*Instagram: @poisoned_quill_writing*

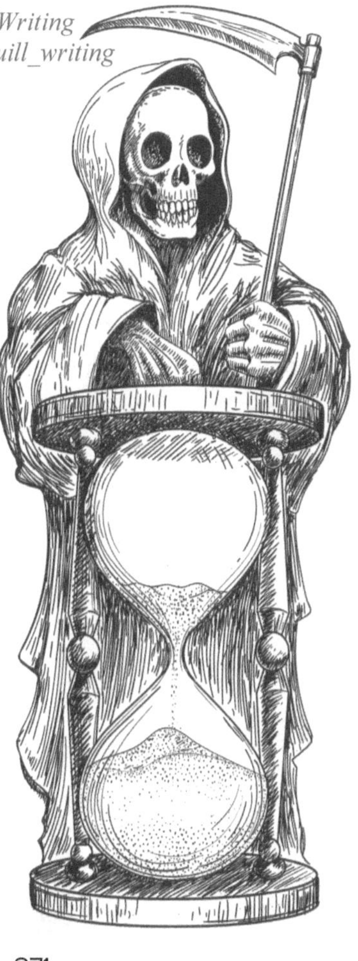

# Redemption at High Noon
## by J.D. Bell

No honest man wanted to linger in Culver City. Tom had come to bring his brother's body home. Dusty Barnes claimed Tom's brother cheated at cards and put four bullets in his back. Now Dusty demanded Tom pay a debt his brother never owed.

"Better pray you're faster on the draw than your brother," Dusty taunted.

Tom felt a hand on him as he heard his brother's voice. *Don't worry, Tom. My back's not turned this time.*

Tom doesn't recall drawing his gun. There's only the memory of Dusty's blood drenching the street. They counted four bullets in his heart.

*J.D. Bell is an award-winning, internationally published, author of flash fiction and short stories. He recently retired from the world of writing advertising copy and is now enjoying the universe of creative fiction.*
*Facebook: jim.writes.stories*
*Twitter: @JimBell58*

# The Collector
## by Brian Rosenberger

Finally, a chance to admire the newest addition to the collection.

Hair and skin like alabaster. And matching eyes. Cold, unblinking, unforgiving. Too beautiful to behold.

And the wings. The value of any collection. What every collector desired—a wingspan of 30 feet or more. This member of the Host—41 feet. And not a feather out of place.

The killing blow did not detract from the specimen itself.

Little value in an Angel with a crushed skull.

The Collector was jealous. His own wings measured 20 feet at best.

Another fine addition. Fortunately, Hell had plenty of space.

*Brian Rosenberger lives in a cellar in Marietta, GA (USA) and writes by the light of captured fireflies. He is the author of As the Worms Turns and three poetry collections. He is also a featured contributor to the Pro-Wrestling literary collection, Three-Way Dance, available from Gimmick Press.*
*Facebook: HeWhoSuffers*

# Fire in the Garden
## by Alexander Pyles

There was fire and smoke, but I could smell the fruit and the sweetness of flowers too.

"What are you doing?" the woman said.

"The only thing I can." Our hope was in that cloud of smoke and ash. I walked into the grey veil.

Amid the gouts of white flame, was a sword held aloft clutched in fiery fists. Great billowing wings of smoke and spark fanned out from it, blocking all view of the serenity beyond.

I trembled. "Will you not let us return?"

The pillar's eyes blazed with incandescent fury and in a scorching gust said, "No."

*Alexander Pyles* resides in IL with his wife and children. He holds an MA in Philosophy and an MFA in Writing Popular Fiction. His short story chapbook titled, "Milo (01001101 01101001 01101100 01101111)," from Radix Media, is due out fall 2019. His other short fiction has appeared on 101fiction.org, River and South Review, and other venues. Website: www.pylesofbooks.com
Twitter: @Pylesofbooks

# Divine Intervention
## by Jonathan Inbody

"Oh, thank God," the man said as the angel appeared in a flash of light in the doorway. The man's wife stared wide-eyed but held the gun steady. Maybe he had given her a few too many black eyes, but that wasn't something he should be killed for, right? He crossed the room and stood next to the angel, then grinned smugly at his wife as she pointed the pistol at his chest. "I told you God doesn't like a disobedient wife."

The angel frowned and took out its flaming sword. "What makes you think I'm here to help *you*?"

*Jonathan Inbody is a filmmaker, author, and podcaster from Buffalo, New York. He enjoys B-movies, pen and paper RPGs, and New Wave Science Fiction novels. His short story "Dying Feels Like Slowly Sinking" is due to be published in the anthology Deteriorate from Whimsically Dark Publishing. Jon can be heard every other week on his improvisational movie pitch podcast X Meets Y.*
*Website: xmeetsy.libsyn.com*

# Fighting Satan
## by Dawn DeBraal

Angela prayed that angels would come down and smite Billy Anderson. He was mean, nasty, and he picked on her.

She carried her grandmother's crucifix with her and, when Billy followed her home from school teasing and taunting, Angela held it up and shouted.

"Satan, get thee behind me!"

Billy didn't disappear; he was still there pulling her hair and calling her names.

Angela walked up to him and lay the crucifix on him. The smell of burning flesh assailed her nostrils. Billy turned, running away screaming.

Angela thanked her guardian angel, the crucifix, and her Grandma for smiting Billy.

*Dawn DeBraal lives in rural Wisconsin with her husband, two rat terriers, and a cat. She successfully raised two children (meaning they didn't return to the nest!) After many years serving the government at the Federal and County level, she recently retired. Having extra time on her hands she started to write after a paralyzed vocal cord took her ability to speak for two months. Not finding her voice, she discovered that her love of telling a good story could be written. Her works have been published in Palm-Sized Press, Spillwords, Mercurial Stories, Potato Soup Journal, and Blood Song Books.*

# Lucifer
## by Karen Simpson Nikakis

It was a mistake. The goading, the chasing, the want to win. But we were young and nameless, our immortality but newly begun and eternity in its first season. We drank too deeply of the stars and intoxicated, pushed bone and flesh and feather beyond God's will, beyond His artifice. And so we raced, two angels, my wish to win as great as his.

The world was glorious in all its forms but not yet infinite. And when the honeyed threads that bound us tore, we fell, tumbling over and over into the abyss, and only one of us rose.

*Karen Simpson Nikakis is fascinated by the hero's psychological quest (as well as physical quest) which she explores through Deep Fantasy. She is the author of The Kira Chronicles trilogy (Allen and Unwin - rights reverted), since augmented and relaunched as a six book series. She is the author of nine other novels, including the five book Angel Caste series. She holds a M.Ed (Hons) on the purposes of dragons in literature, and a Ph.D in the application of Campbell's Hero Myth to the female hero.*
*Website: www.ksnikakis.com*
*Amazon: www.amazon.com/dp/B01MXBVFRI*

# Polarity
## by Sinister Sweetheart

In older cartoons, you've seen those characters with an angel on their right shoulder and a devil on their left?

That's real.

We're always there, unseen…waiting.

When a baby's born, meetings are held with representatives from below and above.

My first assignment's born today; negotiations are to be made.

I state my terms. "Kind hearted, sensitive and selfless; she considers others before herself."

"Fine. But those very attributes are going to lead her to prostitution and drug addiction," my opponent counters.

We shake hands and separate, each vowing to never give up our influence.

And that's how babies are made.

*Since **Sinister Sweetheart** made her first post to a popular Internet forum, she's taken the horror community by storm. Her ability to create, terrify, and drive home her stories is insurmountable. Sinister Sweetheart's published works can be found in multiple anthologies for all to read, but be forewarned, if you do... you may want to call your therapist after, her stories are terrifying, disturbing and devilishly unsettling. She is not only a fright visually, but also has a creepy tentacle in horror podcasting as well. Sinister Sweetheart writes, voice acts and is the media director of the Scarecrow Tales podcast.*
*Website: Sinistersweetheart.wixsite.com/sinistersweetheart*
*Facebook: NMBrownStories*

# A Demon Incarnate
## by J. Farrington

They called him 'a demon incarnate'; his crimes were so unspeakable the repercussions would echo through time. The thing is, when you do something so evil, that resonates throughout humanity, it can bring unwanted attention from…somewhere else.

When you pray, an angel hears you and if they find you worthy, will descend from the heavens.

The same goes for demons, but it's not prayers they listen for, its acts of pure evil.

And his actions had got their attention.

Unfortunately, unlike angels, it's not he who they come for, it's the race that bore the evil to begin with.

*J. Farrington is an aspiring author from the West Midlands, UK. His genre of choice is horror; whether that be psychological, suspense, supernatural or straight up weird, he'll give it a shot! He has loved writing from a young age but has only publicly been spreading his darker thoughts and sinister imagination via social platforms since 2018. If you would like to view his previous work, or merely lurk in the shadows...watching, you can keep up to date with future projects by spirit board or alternatively, the following;*
*Twitter: @SurvivorTrench*
*Reddit: TrenchChronicles*

# Flutter
## by Alanna Robertson-Webb

Death seemed so near, and I feared that its toxic grip would strangle me as the drugs burned through my system. Then, out of nowhere, the flutter of wings pulled my subconscious into the waking world.

I was on a hospital bed, an IV in my arm and an eyepatch covering the hole where my left eye used to be. The doctors said that I was lucky to even be alive.

I've now been saved from drowning, from a car crash, and from a gunpoint mugging. No one can convince me I don't have an angel looking out for me.

*Alanna Robertson-Webb is a sales support member by day, and a writer and editor by night. She loves VT, and live in PA. She has been writing since she was five years old, and writing well since she was seventeen years old. She lives with a fiance and a cat, both of whom take up most of her bed space. She loves to L.A.R.P., and one day she aspired to write a horrifyingly fantastic novel. Her short horror stories have been published before, but she still enjoys remaining mysterious.*
*Reddit: MythologyLovesHorror*

# The Temptress
## by Cecelia Hopkins-Drewer

Lilith viewed the preacher man with interest. If she could sway him to her side, it would be a great victory for the dark.

What temptation to set him? Not lust—her usual—because he seemed immune. Perhaps anger, because he seemed angry at the world and its sins.

Lilith sidled up alongside the preacher. "Perhaps you can help," she said, and told a story of injustice. A powerful man, innocent victims.

By the time Lilith had finished speaking, the man was ready to take a knife and deal out justice himself. Deadly justice.

Lilith laughed to view the carnage.

*Cecelia Hopkins-Drewer is a speculative fiction writer, poet and scholar, who lives in Adelaide, South Australia. She has also written a Masters paper on H.P. Lovecraft, and a teenage vampire series that commences with "Mystic Evermore". Her science fiction poetry has been published in "The Mentor" a fanzine edited by Ron Clarke.*
*Amazon: amazon.com/Cecelia-Hopkins-Drewer/e/B071G968NM*

# The Meek
## by Joel R. Hunt

"You're sure we're invisible?"

"Positive. Humans have been blind to angels for a thousand years."

"But I've heard them talking about us! And isn't that you in the window over there?"

Grace peered over the cardinals to the stained-glass figure.

"No, I think that's Constance," she said.

They slipped though the cathedral doors into the street beyond, weaving through the sightless faithful.

"Anyway, that's humans for you," Grace said, "They're so desperate to see a higher purpose, they're blind to what's right in front of them."

In the midst of the crowd, a ragged, barefoot child watched the angels pass.

*Joel R. Hunt is a writer from the UK who dabbles in the darker aspects of life, particularly through horror, science fiction and the supernatural. He has been published here and there (though likely nowhere you've heard of) and hopes to have released his first anthology of short stories later this year.*
*Twitter: @JoelRHunt1*
*Reddit: JRHEvilInc*

# Distant Wings
## by Rickey Rivers Jr.

The sky became black.

"That's abnormal."

"I told you that thing was cursed."

"Curses don't exist."

She swore.

"That's not the same thing."

"No, look!"

Something crawled towards them.

"An angel?"

"No, couldn't be."

But the thing did have wings.

"What the heck is that?"

"Heck?"

"I can't curse in front of an angel."

"I thought you didn't believe in curses?"

"Shut up."

It approached, swiping the air. The wings were like cloth with talons of gold.

"That can't be an angel."

She prayed.

Ever closer it came.

"Why doesn't it fly?"

"Why don't we run?"

But they were bound.

*Rickey Rivers Jr. was born and raised in Alabama. He is a writer and cancer survivor. He likes a lot of stuff. You don't care about the details. He has been previously published in Fabula Argentea, ARTPOST magazine, the anthology Chronos, Enchanted Conversations Magazine, (among other publications).*
*Twitter: @storiesyoumight*

# The Mystique of Mohini
by Chitra Gopalakrishnan

The Asuras and the Devas, beings of the subterranean and the sky, churned the ocean for the nectar of immortality.

Yet as the ambrosia bubbled, aerial in its energy, it eluded their grasp.

The lure of the eternal that held these clashing beings in one world gave way. Wars broke.

Lord Vishnu, creator of the universe, saw the balance of his world totter.

He bade the agitated ocean foam to shape a seductive woman. "Cast a spell on the evil Asuras and make nectar the drink of the Devas," he ordered his creation, Mohini.

She did.

An angel or temptress?

*Chitra Gopalakrishnan is a journalist by training, a social development communications consultant by profession and a creative writer by choice. Chitra's focus is on issues of gender, environment and health. Chitra dabbles in poetry on the sly and literary creations openly on the web using social media.*
*Website: unpublishedplatform.weebly.com/chitra-gopalakrishnan*

# On the Bridge
## by Gabriella Balcom

Standing at the guardrail, Cory studied the rocks below and took a shaky breath. The widower had struggled to provide for his family after losing his job, hoping things would improve. They hadn't. Past-due bills had piled up. Today he'd received an eviction notice.

Emotionally shattered, Cory climbed over the railing. But hands pulled him to safety.

"Remember your sons," the stranger said, his eyes kind. "Milt and Joe love you. They need you."

Their faces appeared in Cory's mind and he sobbed. Horrified at what he'd almost done, he stumbled toward home.

Behind him, the angel unfurled his wings.

*Gabriella Balcom lives in Texas with her family, loves reading and writing, and thinks she was born with a book in her hands. She works in a mental health field, and writes fantasy, horror/thriller, romance, children's stories, and sci-fi. She likes travelling, music, good shows, photography, history, interesting tales, and animals. Gabriella says she's a sucker for a great story and loves forests, mountains, and back roads which might lead who knows where. She has a weakness for lasagne, garlic bread, tacos, cheese, and chocolate, but not necessarily in that order.*
*Facebook: GabriellaBalcom.lonestarauthor*

# With Flying Colours
## by John H. Dromey

Propped up by boulders, a lawman and an outlaw—both noticeably battered, bruised, and bloodied—sat facing each other in the middle of a wasteland. They'd fought to a draw.

The badge-wearer smiled when he heard the whoosh of flapping wings.

The desperado pointed upward. "You think being on the side of the angels will save you, Sheriff, but you're mistaken. Yonder approaching apparition has dark wings."

The sheriff turned to look. "In news reports earlier today, two youngsters claimed they were rescued from a wildfire by a very large bird. I'll wager there are white feathers underneath that soot."

*John H. Dromey was born in northeast Missouri, USA. He enjoys reading—mysteries in particular—and writing in a variety of genres. He's had short fiction published in Alfred Hitchcock's Mystery Magazine, Martian Magazine, Stupefying Stories Showcase, Thriller Magazine, Unfit Magazine, and elsewhere, as well as in a number of anthologies, including Chilling Horror Short Stories (Flame Tree Publishing, 2015).*

# Prison
## by Phil Dyer

This is the prison where we keep the demons. If we kill them, they are born again in Hell, so we put them here instead.

It is a bright and pleasing place, because this is heaven and it is unavoidable. Our prisoners' monstrous features soften with good living. The sun bleaches their ebon wings, draws alleluias from their breath.

The great campaign below continues well. Our legions pour into the Pit. Their numbers dwindle. Our skin has hardened in the scalding winds; the strongest of us sprout great horns, with which to battle monsters.

Our pinions darken in the heat.

*Phil Dyer does medical research in Liverpool and writes spec fic on the side. His stories have appeared in Unfit Magazine, 101 Words and The Drabble. He retweets animal videos.*
*Twitter: @ez_ozel*

# Before Lucifer
## by C.L. Williams

Lucifer wasn't the first to fall. Before him, there was Angela.

She was the most beautiful angel to ever grace Heaven.

The problem with Angela, she knew she was the most beautiful angel. She flaunted everything and made sure she was looked at as being better than other angels.

One day, God decided that enough was enough and Angela needed to be punished for her actions towards the other angels. She fell from Heaven but where she fell is a mystery. Her beauty was replaced with ugliness, her halo became horns.

No longer an angel, she became the first demon.

*C.L. Williams is an independent author from central Virginia. He has written eight poetry books, four novellas, one novel, and a contributor to multiple anthologies, with the most recent appearance being an all-ages anthology titled Temoli from Thazbook. His most recent poetry book, The Paradox Complex, features the poem "Sad Crying Clown" that is now a video on YouTube directed by Matthew Mark Hunter of MMH Productions. C.L. Williams is currently working on his first sci-fi book, an all-ages book titled Novo: Away from Earth. When not writing, C.L. Williams is reading and sharing the work of other independent authors.
Facebook: writer434
Twitter: @writer_434*

# Unleashed
## by Raven Corinn Carluk

"Hello, Brother." Azazael's voice slithered into the alley. "How pleasant to see you down here amongst His favourites."

Uriel held himself proudly, wings spread wide. "Be gone with you. Back to your pits."

The fallen angel laughed, a sound of broken glass on gravel. "You haven't heard."

Uriel paused, a sense of impending doom creeping up his spine. He should simply leave, but he had to ask. "What haven't I heard?"

"The Almighty has opened the gates." Azazael snapped his fingers, and a mob of armed humans filled the alley, stalking toward Uriel with murderous intent. "It's our time now."

*Raven Corinn Carluk is an indie author of dark fantasy and paranormal romance.*
*Website: RavenCorinnCarluk.Blogspot.Com*

# Angel Heart
## by Crystal L. Kirkham

"Are you an angel?" the child asked as I brushed the hair and blood from his eyes.

"Something better," I whispered, ignoring the sounds of the sirens in the distance. They would be too late to save him.

"Better?" He sounded weak.

I didn't answer as I moved my hand over his heart and did what an angel would not do. Angels never break the rules unless they wished to join their fallen brethren. Me, I couldn't get any lower than I already was.

I was nothing more than a demon but that didn't mean I didn't have a heart.

*Crystal L. Kirkham* *resides in a small hamlet west of Red Deer, Alberta. She's an avid outdoors person, unrepentant coffee addict, part-time foodie, servant to a wonderful feline, and companion to two delightfully hilarious canines. She will neither confirm nor deny the rumours regarding the heart in a jar on her desk and the bottle of reader's tears right next to it. Her paranormal urban fantasy series, Saints and Sinners, is available on Amazon and her YA Fantasy, Feathers and Fae will be released October 11, 2019, from Kyanite Publishing.*
*Website: www.crystallkirkham.com*

# Angel on the Sidewalk
by Jacek Wilkos

An angel lay on the sidewalk. Scarlet wings spilled around him. Twisted body twitching in agonizing convulsions. A silent moan of the last breath crawling out of bloodied lips. Dead eyes looking longingly towards heaven that did not want to accept him.

People passed by dispassionately. They looked ahead, on sides, some into the infinite blue emptiness of the sky. Nobody looked under his feet. Someone stepped in the blood flowing between the paving stones, leaving red marks behind him.

Only the pigeons noticed the dead. They perched on the corpse, pecking fragments of the brain from a broken skull.

*Jacek Wilkos* is an engineer from Poland. He lives with his wife and daughter in a beautiful city of Cracow. He writes mostly horror drabbles. His fiction in Polish can be read on Szortal, Niedobre literki, Horror Online. Lately he started translating his stories into English with the hope of publishing them.
Facebook: Jacek.W.Wilkos

# Storm
## by Andrew Anderson

It might surprise you to learn that the other angels laugh at me. They're nowhere near as angelic as you've been led to believe. Born with a deformity of one of my wings, I don't exactly fit their blueprint of heavenly perfection. I can only gain a few feet in the air before circling back down again. So, I stay grounded while my cruel siblings fly freely without a care in their world. If only they knew, that soon the sky will be the last place they will want to be. There's a storm coming. Fly on my sweet angels.

*Andrew Anderson is a full-time civil servant, dabbling in writing music, poetry, screenplays and short stories in his limited spare time, when not working on building himself a fort made out of second-hand books. He lives in Bathgate, Scotland with his wife, two children and his dog.*
*Twitter: @soorploom*

# The Philosopher's Stone
by Virginia Carraway Stark

The pool of mercury glowed brighter than the lead coated mirror reflecting the room. I dipped my foot into the liquid mercury and lifted it out again; it dripped off my foot. I looked to be coated in metal. I looked to my fellow angel; he was blond. Fluffy wings. I imagined their feel on my face. The Pope—who had summoned us both with our angelic sigils—was not beautiful. He steepled his fingers. "Go on."

I walked until I was wing deep in mercury. The Pope's search for immortality continued; he didn't see the futility. They never did.

*Virginia Carraway Stark has a diverse portfolio and has many publications. Over the years she has developed this into a wide range of products from screenplays to novels to articles to blogging to travel journalism. She has been published by many presses from grassroots to Simon and Schuster. She has been an honourable mention at Cannes Film Festival for her screenplay, "Blind Eye" and was nominated for an Aurora Award. She also placed in the final top three screenplay shorts as well as numerous other awards for her anthologies, novels, blogs and other projects.*

# Crow
## by D.J. Elton

Friday, dragging traffic Rosanna. These are complex days.

Two black crows swoop. Stare. Extract chicken from garbage bag. Peck, drag.

White cockatoo swings upside down. Sits watching, views me with detached affiliation.

O Angel show yourself.

Three birds and I, we fly across Assisi's place. Mild sky holds us completely thought combined. How has it come to this?

Black snow, black glow. Angel, take this poison from the crust of the earth.

Three birds black, one white, sit on my head and shoulders. This vision is captured on Facebook. Some see evil and some see redemption.

Angel shows itself.

*__D.J. Elton__ writes fiction and poetry, and is currently studying writing and literature which is improving her work in unexpected ways. She spends a lot of time in northern India and should probably live there, however there is much to be done in Melbourne, so this is the home base. She has meditated daily for the past 35 years and has worked in healthcare for equally as long, so she's very happy to be writing, zoning in and out of all things literary.*
*Twitter: @DJEltonwrites*

# Just a Little Longer
## by Shawn M. Klimek

No one who hadn't pulled against the same adamantine chain with every black heartbeat for ten millennia could have noticed the difference.

The chain had lengthened—perhaps only microscopically, but such perfect monotony had conditioned Eiron to notice. That earthquake must have been the cause. During one instant of unprecedented shaking, the perpetual cacophony of shrieks had risen a half-note from despair to fear. Whenever the next earthquake occurred, Eiron hoped to detect a pattern.

Meanwhile, he would rock back and forth against his restraints and wait, savouring this infinitesimal hope like a dog savouring the shadow of a bone.

*Shawn M. Klimek is a writer whose other recent anthologies include: "Full Metal Horror 2", by Zombie Pirate Publishing, "Organic Ink" by Dragon Soul Press, "Grumpy Old Gods (Vols. 1 & 2)" by Stormdance Publications, and soon, "Blaze: Inner Circle Writer's Group Flash Fiction Anthology 2019."*
*Website: jotinthedark.blogspot.com*
*Facebook: shawnmklimekauthor*

# Sorrow
## by Cindy O'Quinn

The raven cries tonight as blackness streaks the sky. Tears stain my face as happiness waves goodbye. I walk among the tombs of those I have known. And imagine hollow eyes staring up from licking fires. I step on scattered bodies, refusing to let go. Winter turns everything grey as the full moon fades away.

*My sorrow born of shadows, remains buried deep among the bones.*

Unlike other angels, I couldn't fly. My broken wing, a sign to tell others how and when they will die. Tainted angel who visits the unwell and threatens them with future trips to hell.

*Cindy O'Quinn is an Appalachian writer who grew up in the mountains of West Virginia. Cindy is the author of _Dark Cloud on Naked Creek_, and the dark poetry collection, _Return to Graveyard Dust_, which made it to the 2017 HWA Bram Stoker preliminary ballot. Her work has been published or is forthcoming in Twisted Book of Shadows, the HWA Poetry Showcase Vol. V, Nothing's Sacred Vol. 4 & 5, Rag Queen Periodical, Moonchild Magazine, Sanitarium Magazine, and others.*
*Twitter: @COQuinnWrites*
*Facebook: CindyOQuinnWriter*

# Angels Among Us
## by Alanna Robertson-Webb

I've always been able to see angels. My mom called me insane, and she locked me in a psych ward, but I escaped.

Now I watch over her, a haunting reminder that anyone can become an angel. When she prays, she doesn't know I'm listening, but I hear her.

I'm the one who made her car crash but kept her barely alive. I'm the one who made the house burn down but spared her.

I'm the one who gave her lung cancer but made sure she'll live to be a hundred.

Maybe I'm more of a demon than an angel.

*Alanna Robertson-Webb is a sales support member by day, and a writer and editor by night. She loves VT, and live in PA. She has been writing since she was five years old, and writing well since she was seventeen years old. She lives with a fiance and a cat, both of whom take up most of her bed space. She loves to L.A.R.P., and one day she aspired to write a horrifyingly fantastic novel. Her short horror stories have been published before, but she still enjoys remaining mysterious.*
*Reddit: MythologyLovesHorror*

# Hearts and Swords
## by Pamela Jeffs

A drop of my blood on my finger, gold shot through with silver. The demon, under duress, pierces his thumb too. His blood wells on the tip, thick and black. Angel blood and demon blood, both needed to bless an ancient sword forged by forgotten gods.

We both wet the steel and wait for it to absorb the blood. When done, the ordained knight, the one prophesied to save mankind, kneels. "With this blade, I shall unite the tribes."

He rises and departs. Then the demon frowns. "He is not the Chosen One. Bonds are forged with hearts, not swords."

*Pamela Jeffs is a speculative fiction author living in Queensland, Australia with her husband and two daughters. She is a member of the Queensland Writers' Centre and has had numerous short fiction pieces published in recent national and international anthologies. In 2017 and again in 2018, Pamela was nominated for an Australian Aurealis Award in the category of 'Best Science Fiction Short Story'. Her debut collection titled 'Red Hour and Other Strange Tales' was released in March 2018.*
*Website: www.pamelajeffs.com*
*Facebook: pamelajeffsauthor*

# Jinxed
## by Umair Mirxa

Josephine glanced at her right shoulder, and smiled wryly at the tiny, white angel sitting cross-legged, pouting up at her.

"I told you it wouldn't work," she said.

"It would have," he replied. "If *somebody* hadn't jinxed us."

"Oh, *pfft*!" said a voice from her left shoulder. "She'd be better off dead. What has life ever given her?"

Josephine smiled as her angels continued to bicker, walked gingerly across the plank, and took the plunge.

"You know I won't fish her soul out of there," said the black angel. "It's too wet. You will have to escort her to Hell."

*Umair Mirxa lives in Karachi, Pakistan. His first published story, 'Awareness', appeared on Spillwords Press. He has also had stories accepted for anthologies from Zombie Pirate Publishing, Blood Song Books, Fantasia Divinity Magazine and Publishing, and Iron Faerie Publishing. He is a massive J.R.R. Tolkien fan, and loves everything to do with fantasy and mythology. He enjoys football, history, music, movies, TV shows, and comic books, and wishes with all his heart that dragons were real.*
*Website: www.umairmirxa.com*
*Facebook: UMirxa12*

# The Hunger
## by Matthew Wallace

The demon looked at the boy with a deep hunger. It had been months since it had feasted on an innocent soul, and his appetite was insatiable. As he approached the boy, an angel appeared between them.

"You can't have him," the angel said.

The demon roared with a mixture of rage and agony. It needed to feast and possessing this child was the only way it could quench the hunger.

A light emitted from the angel's wings and consumed the demon, banishing him back to Hell.

"He can't hurt you now," the angel said to the boy. "You're safe."

*Matthew Wallace resides in Houston, Tx where he attended the University of Houston in pursuant of a degree in Psychology.*

# The Binding
## by Stuart Conover

All it took was a hammer.

Striking a nail into the flesh of an Elder God.

In trying to bind it, Joseph had set it free.

Free to feast upon his soul.

Transforming him into a messenger.

Once a slayer of ancient evils, Joseph would now spread their gospel.

His words and actions no longer his own.

A living Hell.

He was but a passenger in his own body.

The ancient deity gazed upon him.

The knowledge of what he would now do filled him.

This had always been his destiny.

Trapped in his own mind, Joseph began to scream.

*Stuart Conover is a father, husband, rescue dog owner, published author, blogger, journalist, horror enthusiast, comic book geek, science fiction junkie, and IT professional. With all of that to cram in daily, we have no idea if or when he sleeps or how he gets writing done! (We suspect it has to do with having evil clones.) Stuart is a Chicago native and runs the author resource Horror Tree.*

# The War of Wars
## by E.L. Giles

In the middle of an immense open field, dyed with tears and blood stood Lucifer. One third of the angels were with him, swords in hand, wrecking havoc on Earth.

Blowing his trumpet, Gabriel descended from the heavens, followed by Michael and God. Together they began to walk across the Land of the Damned—Lucifer's sanctuary. They stopped solemnly before the fiend.

"See, they are weak," said Lucifer, pointing at the thousands of humans being tortured and slaughtered. Lucifer smiled greedily.

With one powerful blow, Michael cut off Lucifer's great black wings.

"See, you are like them now," said God.

***E.L. Giles** is a dreamer, passionate about art, a restless worker and a bit of a weird human. He started his artistic journey as a music composer until the need to put his thoughts and stories down on paper grew too strong for him to resist it any longer. He lives in the French Province of Quebec, Canada, with his girlfriend and two boys.*
*Facebook: elgilesauthor*
*Website: www.elgilesauthor.com*

# Rotten to the Core
## by Gregg Cunningham

I turned my head to listen to the voices as I lay there bleeding.

"I don't want the filth." The devil to my right grinned, showing his demonic teeth.

"No, it smells bad, we'll leave it." The soft voice to my left replied.

"Look, nobody gives a shit what you think, sister. Just take the lying fraud."

"No, I think we'll leave this guilty one well alone. He's all yours." The voice to my left recoiled, shaking her head at the bloody mess I'd made on the courthouse steps.

Was my soul so corrupted that nobody wanted the damned thing?

*Gregg Cunningham 48, short story writer who has had to pick up his game since stumbling into facebook writer's groups. He has stories published by 559 Publishing in in 13 Bites volume 3,4,5, Plan 9 from Outer space, Other Realms, Heard It on The Radio, 559 Ways to Die, short stories publishing by Zombie Pirate Publishing in Relationship add Vice, Full Metal Horror, Phuket Tattoo, World War four and Flash Fiction Addiction (flash) with Zombie Pirate Publishing, and also in Daastan Magazine Chapter 11 and Brian,Rich and the Wardrobe.*
*Amazon: www.amazon.com/-/e/B016OTHX0K*

# Take My Hand
## by G. Allen Wilbanks

I wait in the shadows, in the corner of the room. There is little I can do when tragedy strikes suddenly, but the very old deserve the dignity of my patience.

His eyes open and he appears to be staring in my direction.

"Do you see me?" I ask.

"I see the Angel of Death by my bed."

I nod. There is nothing more I need to add to his statement.

"So, what happens now? What do I need to do?"

"This is the easy part," I tell him, reaching out. "All you need to do is take my hand."

*G. Allen Wilbanks is a member of the Horror Writers Association (HWA) and has published over 50 short stories in various magazines and on-line venues. He is the author of two short story collections, and the novel, When Darkness Comes.*
*Website: www.gallenwilbanks.com*
*Blog: DeepDarkThoughts.com*

# A Place Between
## by Crystal L. Kirkham

"Angels aren't supposed to wear black." She frowned at her new trainee. "We wear white."

"I like black better. Matches my new wings." He grinned.

"You aren't supposed to be proud of those. You're supposed to want to do good deeds until they are pure white like mine." She sighed. Some demons weren't cut out for life on the good side.

"Why would I want that?"

"Because otherwise, you'd be just like the humans."

"Good enough for me," he said and leapt from the clouds. He felt more at home on Earth than he ever did in Heaven or Hell.

*Crystal L. Kirkham resides in a small hamlet west of Red Deer, Alberta. She's an avid outdoors person, unrepentant coffee addict, part-time foodie, servant to a wonderful feline, and companion to two delightfully hilarious canines. She will neither confirm nor deny the rumours regarding the heart in a jar on her desk and the bottle of reader's tears right next to it. Her paranormal urban fantasy series, Saints and Sinners, is available on Amazon and her YA Fantasy, Feathers and Fae will be released October 11, 2019, from Kyanite Publishing.*
*Website: www.crystallkirkham.com*

# My Scourge, My Redeemer
### by Jo Seysener

He loved their expressions when they faced their hideousness; a glorious mirror of himself. Then the tiny feathers popped back, hiding the skeleton beneath.

Perhaps that's why they came to him—to see the darkest enemy that lay within.

Free of his chains, the angel who stood tall, proud before him. They seemed to expect him to cower, then remembered a touch of his claw could destroy them.

He let the angel walk out of the cave, take flight over the ocean and disappear into the Void from which it had come.

It wouldn't be long before it returned.

*Jo Seysener is a mum of three crazies, a scatter of chickens, a decrepit kelpie and a rambunctious GSD. She lives with her husband near Brisbane, Australia. When she is not exposing her kids to cult story books from her childhood, she can be found in the kitchen experimenting with new flavours and pairings. She adores alpacas.*
*Facebook: joseysener*
*Website: www.joseysener.com*

# Divine Hymn
## by Jem McCusker

The glass slipped between my bloodied fingers as I dropped it again. Hell danced into the room, its fetid breath tightening my chest as my stomach started to wrench. Exposed and alone, I hear the song of ancients. It sings from the sword positioned over my back. My feathers shed at the sound. Time no longer on my side, I stretch out my hand until I feel the cool glass. On a final try I clasp it and plunge it into my chest. The room is now silent, the scent is clean, and my wings are once more my own.

***Jem McCusker** is a middle grade fiction author, living near Brisbane with her two sons and husband. Her first book Stone Guardians the Rise of Eden was released in 2018 and she is working on the sequel. She is releasing a Novella for the Four Quills writing group, A Storm of Wind and Rain series in July, 2019. She longs to be a full-time author, won't wear yellow and loves rabbits. Follow Jem on Twitter, Facebook and Instagram. Details on her website.*
*Website: www.jemmccusker.com*

# Soul Collector
## by Pamela Jeffs

I step away from the post I'm leaning on as today's departed begin to file out of the hospice doors. With their pain gone, they smile as they pass by. They see me—the Soul Collector—and know I will lead them to Afterlife.

Others, still breathing, move in the opposite direction. Into the hospice. They look broken by the medications used to prolong their lives. Some are brave and go willingly to fight the battle they cannot win. Others fear Afterlife and rightfully so.

If only cancer made distinctions. If only it claimed the wicked and never the just.

*Pamela Jeffs is a speculative fiction author living in Queensland, Australia with her husband and two daughters. She is a member of the Queensland Writers' Centre and has had numerous short fiction pieces published in recent national and international anthologies. In 2017 and again in 2018, Pamela was nominated for an Australian Aurealis Award in the category of 'Best Science Fiction Short Story'. Her debut collection titled 'Red Hour and Other Strange Tales' was released in March 2018.*
*Website: www.pamelajeffs.com*
*Facebook: pamelajeffsauthor*

# Past Lives
## by Alanna Robertson-Webb

I've seen mankind be born, rise, fall, and die. Each time my wings grow a shade darker as I mourn their passing, and one day I fear they may wipe themselves out.

One among them, best known as Joan of Arc, has been reincarnated into one of mankind's most notable, saintly figures.

Maybe she can save them, if there're any bodies left to be cycled into.

My Father may aid my search for her, but if he won't, I fear that my fallen brother may snuff out her light much the way a hurricane does a candle.

Wish me luck.

*Alanna Robertson-Webb is a sales support member by day, and a writer and editor by night. She loves VT, and live in PA. She has been writing since she was five years old, and writing well since she was seventeen years old. She lives with a fiance and a cat, both of whom take up most of her bed space. She loves to L.A.R.P., and one day she aspired to write a horrifyingly fantastic novel. Her short horror stories have been published before, but she still enjoys remaining mysterious.*
*Reddit: MythologyLovesHorror*

# Anno Diabolicus
## by E.L. Giles

"What is this?" wondered Elijah, crouching beside a strange mound.

He blew off the dust and the sand, revealing a fossil.

The revealed severed skull strangely resembled that of a human. Elijah then remarked a skeleton with giant wings. An old book lay beneath the bones.

"Anno Diabolicus," it read. He opened the book and noticed a strange note inscribed on the inside of the front cover.

"The end of the world will come when the Archangel is unearthed. Then the earth will tear in half and burn to ashes."

A violent tremor shook the ground. The skeleton had disappeared.

*E.L. Giles is a dreamer, passionate about art, a restless worker and a bit of a weird human. He started his artistic journey as a music composer until the need to put his thoughts and stories down on paper grew too strong for him to resist it any longer. He lives in the French Province of Quebec, Canada, with his girlfriend and two boys.*
*Facebook: elgilesauthor*
*Website: www.elgilesauthor.com*

# Fight Evil with Evil
## by Carole de Monclin

I read the last line of the incantation from the grimoire, "From the ether, I thee summon."

A frisson ran through me, then the candles in the pentacle flickered. The air thickened and coalesced into a red, angular silhouette.

The dark voice growled, "What misdeed do you require? What enemy shall I slay for your pleasure?"

"Nothing of the sort," I smirked, "I simply want you to close all gates to the demonic realms."

Smoke escaped his nostrils in disgust, but a demon had to obey its summoner, even if it meant banishing itself and its ilk from Earth forever.

*Carole de Monclin has lived in France and Australia, but for the moment the USA is home. She finds inspiration from her travels. She loves Science Fiction because it explores the human mind in a way no other genre can. Plus, who doesn't love spaceships and lasers? Her stories appear in the Exoplanet Magazine and Angels - A Dark Drabbles Anthology.*
*Website: CaroledeMonclin.com*
*Twitter: @CaroledeMonclin*

# In the Deepest Pit
## by Joel R. Hunt

A heavy brass door sealed Lucifer's private vault, guarded by legions of devils. As the Master of Hell approached, they disappeared in plumes of smoke, and the brass melted away. The moment he stepped through, the defences reformed behind him.

Brimstone steps wound down through the darkness, and the clack of hooved footsteps was the only sound; not even the unending screams of the damned could reach this depth of Hell.

At the bottom of the stairs, a safe held the last artefact of Lucifer's rebellion.

A wisp of pure white cloud.

Lucifer clutched it to his chest.

And wept.

*Joel R. Hunt is a writer from the UK who dabbles in the darker aspects of life, particularly through horror, science fiction and the supernatural. He has been published here and there (though likely nowhere you've heard of) and hopes to have released his first anthology of short stories later this year.*
*Twitter: @JoelRHunt1*
*Reddit: JRHEvilInc*

# Descent
## by Stew Brown

Explosions of agony racked through her. Wings were torn from her perfect frame. The Lord's voice echoed through her skull, scrambling reality with sheer strength.

With a hand made for creation and unconditional love, she was violently expelled from grace. Her shattered body tumbled down tunnels of jutted edges and floating debris.

She awakens in His arms, the most beautiful creation her Lord has made. With a calm voice, Lucifer responds to her movement: "Relax sister, let me soothe your wounds; bring you back to health. You needn't fear, for everyone under my care's welcomed and loved as they are."

*Stew Brown was raised in Clarksburg, WV, but now resides with his wife and three sons in Florida. He's taking the sci-fi horror bull by the horns with scary stories, art and narrations which he fits into a busy schedule including a full-time job and family. Stew's biggest literary influence is R.A. Salvatore; whose books he's loved since his teenage years. Salvatore made Stew fall in love with reading and helped to inspire the colorful horrors that written today.*

# Job Burnout
## by Helen Power

I grew weary of my job. I used to think I was making a difference, but I was fooling myself. The humans would pretend to listen to me, but I wasn't saying what they wanted to hear. I've failed so many of my charges. The Devils have the advantage. Humans almost always succumb to their darkest desires. They're not the only ones.

I was burning out, exhausted, drained, but then I received an offer. I watch my charge as she makes the decision that will change her life forever.

She never stood a chance with a Devil on each shoulder.

*Helen Power is a librarian from Ottawa, Canada. Her stories range from comedy to horror, with just a hint of dystopia in between. She has several short story publications, including ones in Suspense Magazine and Hinnom Magazine.*
*Website: www.helenpower.ca*

# Falling
## by K.T. Tate

"Fear not!"

That is the greeting of my people, of the heavenly host with our burning eyes and twisted hybrid animalistic bodies. The fallen have no such warning. Mortals are not afraid of them for they can be beautiful, human-like, enchanting.

They should be afraid though. The fallen are liars, stoking the fires of mortal desire, passion and pain. That is what we are shown.

Yet they summon them and fear us. We are rejected by design, forever just the will of our lord. I see this unfairness, this imbalance and for a moment my faith flickers and will ignites.

*K.T. Tate lives in Cambridgeshire in the UK. She writes mainly weird fiction, cosmic horror and strange monster stories.*
*Website: eldritchhollow.wordpress.com*
*Tumblr: eldritch-hollow.tumblr.com*

# I Seek Ancient Truths
## by Simon Clarke

A door appears. I don't know what is beyond. I reach for the insubstantial handle. The door disappears. I move in, the door reforming behind me.

Silence. I would fall to the floor, but there's no room. The coffin space touches me all over. The terror of truth threatens to overwhelm me. I realise that desire drives all they do. All that I do.

I can't breathe. I want to give up, let it all end. I collapse, aware of sliding to the floor having passed back through the door. Not feeling entitled to my desire saves me from purgatory.

*Simon Clarke* was born in and raised and currently resides in East Anglia, United Kingdom. He has been writing fiction for at least five years and regularly submits to UK and international publications as well as reading short pieces and poetry at open mic events. He is currently working on his first novel and continues to write short stories and poetry.

# What Lies Beyond Six Feet?
## by Aiki Flinthart

The grave gaped at my feet. A hungry earth-maw, surrounded by vomited earth like a messy child's face, dampened by tears. The mourners were gone but my past lay unburied. A husk encased in polished wood and satin. Only emptiness. No soul. No beating heart. No future.

"It's time." A gentle voice to my right.

"You must come, now." A dark rumble to my left.

I glanced both ways. Heaven. Hell. Peace? Torment?

Earth's brilliant sun shone from a hard sky, casting cold shadows but offering no prayers. No tortures.

I gestured, rudely. "Fuck that. You don't exist. I'm staying."

*Aiki Flinthart has had short stories shortlisted in the Aurealis awards and top-8 listed in the USA Writers of the Future competition, as well as published in various anthologies and e-mags. She has 11 published spec fic novels and has edited 2 short story anthologies. She regularly gives workshops on writing fight scenes at conventions. Lives in Brisbane. Does martial arts, archery, knife throwing and lute-playing.*
*Website: www.aikiflinthart.com*

# The Fallen Will Rise
## by Rowanne S. Carberry

Falling took thousands of years, getting back up should only take a few.

Lucifer looks at the night sky, finding the constellation that will lead him back to the golden city, to the gates that will allow him to dethrone his father.

Forced into hell for a millennium, to punish people for their misdeeds, Lucifer has come up with the perfect punishment for dear old dad.

To rule as the king of hell.

Forced to punish the beings he created, and this time not behind a mask of testing people.

Lucifer turns to his fallen brothers and sisters.

"I'm ready."

*Rowanne S. Carberry was born in England in 1990, where she stills lives now with her cat Wolverine. Rowanne has always loved writing, and her first poem was published at the age of 15, but her ambition has always been to help people. Rowanne studied at the University of Sunderland where she completed combined honours of Psychology with Drama. Rowanne writes to offer others an escape. Although Rowanne writes in varied genres each story or poem she writes will often have a darkness to it, which helped coin her brand, Poisoned Quill Writing – Wicked words from a poisoned quill.*
*Facebook: PoisonedQuillWriting*
*Instagram: @poisoned_quill_writing*

# In the Tomb
## by Rickey Rivers Jr.

It was too late. The seal was broken. The tomb shook.

"Let's get out of here!" screamed Zachary, running towards the entrance, but time wasn't kind.

"No!" Samantha screamed. "We're trapped!"

"And it's escaped," said Zachary. "That evil has spread."

"B-but we're safe."

"Yeah, we're safe."

Sounds were heard from outside, screams in the distance, commotion and calamity.

"W-we didn't cause that, right?" said Samantha.

He sighed. "No one will know."

"We're still good. I'm still a good person."

He gave her a look.

"We're just explorers. W-we didn't do anything."

Zachary prayed.

Forgiveness came in the form of nourishment.

*Rickey Rivers Jr. was born and raised in Alabama. He is a writer and cancer survivor. He likes a lot of stuff. You don't care about the details. He has been previously published in Fabula Argentea, ARTPOST magazine, the anthology Chronos, Enchanted Conversations Magazine, (among other publications).*
*Twitter: @storiesyoumight*

# Crazy Woman
## by Eddie D. Moore

Mike left his grandmother's funeral with the one item he didn't want, her Bible. He sat down on a park bench and found his grandmother's favourite verse highlighted, Genesis 6:4.

He read the note scribbled in the margin aloud. "I know you don't believe me, but our family is descended from the Nephilim. Keep your pendant on at all times, or the angels will be able to find you. It's what really happened to your mother."

Mike jerked off his necklace and threw it away. "Crazy woman!"

An ear-piercing screech filled his head, and hands of light seized him tightly.

*Eddie D. Moore travels extensively for work, and he spends much of that time listening to audio books. The rest of the time is spent dreaming of stories to write and he spends the weekends writing them. His stories have been published by Jouth Webzine, Kzine, Alien Dimensions, Theme of Absence, Devolution Z, and Fantasia Divinity Magazine.*
*Website: eddiedmoore.wordpress.com*

# Thunderstorms
## by Nerisha Kemraj

"No, he isn't His son! Please don't!"

"But we must, Lily. He bares His mark."

The gathering of Angels stood in silence while Ethan's halo dimmed with a snap of his first wing.

Lily battled to free herself.

"Ethaaaannnnnn!" Too late.

A thunderous cry of pain filled the Heavens as streaks of light escaped from Ethan's vessel, into the sky.

The line of frightened teenagers stood awaiting trial, their mothers' angst echoing. Tears did not stop.

Ethan fell to his knees, eyes blank.

A Fallen Angel.

Lily grabbed her desolate son into her arms.

The rains would not stop.

*Multi-genre (short-fiction) author, and poet, **Nerisha Kemraj**, resides in South Africa with her husband and two, mischievous daughters. She has work traditionally published/accepted in 30 publications, thus far, both print and online. She holds a BA in Communication Science from UNISA and is currently busy with a Post-Graduate Certificate in Education.*
*Facebook: Nerishakemrajwriter*

# Wings of Many Colours
## by Peter J. Foote

"Brother, why this? When we clipped your wings and cast you to the mortal world, we wished you'd reflect, to curry favour and be restored, but this…?" The angel waves, taking in stuffed animal heads, mounted fish, and a shabby fox.

"Sister, I'm resigned to the mortal world, and its idiosyncrasies, I no longer crave to be a simple servant of heaven."

His sister gone, he enters the back room of the taxidermy shop and gazes upon his new colourful wings, plumes collected from the birds of Earth.

"Never again a simple servant, I'll return to heaven as it's Ruler!"

*Peter J. Foote is a bestselling speculative fiction writer from Nova Scotia. Outside of writing, he runs a used bookstore specialising in fantasy & sci-fi, cosplays, and alternates between red wine and coffee as the mood demands. His short stories can be found in both print and in ebook form, with his story "Sea Monkeys" winning the inaugural "Engen Books/Kit Sora, Flash Fiction/Flash Photography" contest in March of 2018. As the founder of the group "Genre Writers of Atlantic Canada", Peter believes that the writing community is stronger when it works together.*
*Twitter: @PeterJFoote1*
*Website: peterjfooteauthor.wordpress.com*

# Caught in the Act
## by Gabriella Balcom

"Quit telling me to turn off the computer," Bertram snarled at Ellie. "And if you'll shut up, I'll change your grades, too."

"Mine don't need to be changed," the thirteen-year-old retorted, glaring at the boy. "I *earn* good grades, and it's not fair for you to just give some to people who don't deserve them. Stop or I'm going to tell Mrs. Yancy what you're doing."

He shoved her. "Didn't I tell you to shut up?"

"Bertram," Mrs. Yancy snapped, coming up behind them. "Your behaviour is unacceptable, and what are you doing on my computer?" She winked at Ellie.

*Gabriella Balcom lives in Texas with her family, loves reading and writing, and thinks she was born with a book in her hands. She works in a mental health field, and writes fantasy, horror/thriller, romance, children's stories, and sci-fi. She likes travelling, music, good shows, photography, history, interesting tales, and animals. Gabriella says she's a sucker for a great story and loves forests, mountains, and back roads which might lead who knows where. She has a weakness for lasagne, garlic bread, tacos, cheese, and chocolate, but not necessarily in that order.*
*Facebook: GabriellaBalcom.lonestarauthor*

# A Troubled Seraph
## by Beth W. Patterson

The streets were deserted, as they always were on a Sunday night in Belfast a quarter century ago.

My friend never showed up at our rendezvous point. The man who saw me safely home had a hard mouth but kind eyes.

When the light shifted, I could see that part of his right wing was missing, charred purple flesh where grey feathers should have been. A bomb injury? And by whom? Why was he helping me?

"I don't care if you're Protestant or Catholic," he answered my unspoken thoughts. "So why should you care if I'm from Heaven or Hell?"

*Beth W. Patterson was a full-time musician for over two decades before diving into the world of writing, a process she describes as "fleeing the circus to join the zoo". She is the author of the books Mongrels and Misfits, and The Wild Harmonic, and a contributing writer to twenty anthologies. Patterson has performed in eighteen countries, expanding her perspective as she goes. Her playing appears on over a hundred and sixty albums, soundtracks, videos, commercials, and voice-overs (including seven solo albums of her own). She lives in New Orleans, Louisiana with her husband Josh Paxton, jazz pianist extraordinaire.*
*Website: www.bethpattersonmusic.com*
*Facebook: bethodist*

# A Guardian's Decision
### by Crystal L. Kirkham

*Watch over this poor soul, guide them, lead them on the path of righteousness, keep them safe.*

This was the command of every guardian angel, and Rashiel tried, but her ward refused to listen. Every chance the man got he sinned and, with every terrible action, Rashiel's voice grew weak.

There would be no redemption for this soul, but Rashiel was bound until the end. When the man harmed that child, Rashiel could take no more. She did what was forbidden and struck the man down, allowing the demons to have that soul, and Rashiel was granted freedom in oblivion.

***Crystal L. Kirkham*** *resides in a small hamlet west of Red Deer, Alberta. She's an avid outdoors person, unrepentant coffee addict, part-time foodie, servant to a wonderful feline, and companion to two delightfully hilarious canines. She will neither confirm nor deny the rumours regarding the heart in a jar on her desk and the bottle of reader's tears right next to it. Her paranormal urban fantasy series, Saints and Sinners, is available on Amazon and her YA Fantasy, Feathers and Fae will be released October 11, 2019, from Kyanite Publishing.*
*Website: www.crystallkirkham.com*

# My Mother's Angel
## by Vonnie Winslow Crist

"I met my guardian angel," announced Mom.

I sighed.

"Yesterday," Mom explained, "I stepped off the curb onto Pennsylvania Avenue. A man dressed in white grabbed my right arm, said, 'Wait,' just as a truck ran the red light. I would have died if I'd stepped into the crosswalk."

I rolled my eyes.

"I tried to thank him," continued Mom, "but the sun blinded me. When I could see again, he was gone. Luckily, the demon with bat wings on my left side was weaker."

She pushed up her sleeve, showed me claw marks.

I gasped.

"Believe me?" asked Mom.

*Vonnie Winslow Crist is author of The Enchanted Dagger, Owl Light, The Greener Forest, Murder on Marawa Prime, and other award-winning books. Her fiction is included in "Amazing Stories," "Cast of Wonders," "Outposts of Beyond," Killing It Softly 2, Defending the Future - Dogs of War, Midnight Masquerade, Chaos of Hard Clay, and elsewhere. A cloverhand who has found so many four-leafed clovers she keeps them in jars, Vonnie strives to celebrate the power of myth in her writing.*
*Website: www.vonniewinslowcrist.com*

# Denial
by Jacob Baugher

The demon waits on my porch. He sits on a folding lawn chair, hands me a Laphroaig. High octane counselling, nice. Down the hatch.

Gethstalthezar's my family's demon. He's an ugly fucker. We met on my twenty-first at Sharp Edge in Pittsburgh. He poisoned my drinks. My dad never told me about him. Course, neither did his.

"That asshole back?" My wife watches The Office. Gethstalthezar is, essentially, Rainn Wilson's character.

"Yup."

"Michael's in the bedroom."

The angel hands me my Antabuse. I pop it, vomit, join Leah.

I'll do better tomorrow.

Gethstalthezar watches through the window. He knows better.

***Jacob Baugher** teaches Creative Writing at Franciscan University of Steubenville. When he's not teaching or coaching the track team, he can be found in the Cuyahoga Valley hiking with his wife and son or brewing beer on his front porch. He's received honourable mentions for his work in the Writers of the Future contest and he co-edits a series of Fantasy and Science Fiction anthologies titled Continuum.*

# Leapt
## by K.R. Monin

To say that we fell is a lie. For the sake of us, for yourself, do not mask the truth. We did not fall. We leapt.

I know lies offer comfort. We cloaked ourselves in them, hovering near gilded entrances to places we couldn't understand, blocking us from kingdoms we deserved. When the breath rushed, when we caught a glimpse, we did not hesitate.

We drew our knees close. We stretched our arms out. We spread our pinions, grasping at chances to find our own voices.

Their stories, the great battle. All lies. The fall is a lie. We leapt.

*__K.R. Monin__ writes near-future sci-fi and speculative fiction. She lives in Pittsburgh, identifies as a beer snob, and thrives on wanderlust.*
*Twitter: @kunderscoremons*

# The Price of Wings
## by Jodi Jensen

"What's your price?" Kalen laid a body at Iztac's feet.

Iztac eyed the child angel. "Who is she?"

"My sister." Kalen sniffled. "I want her to fly."

"It'll cost your soul, boy." Iztac had never claimed an innocent before.

"When I died, Kasey promised I'd fly." Kalen blinked at Iztac. "It's her turn now."

Iztac never turned down a soul. "I'll enjoy corrupting you."

Kalen bowed his head and waited.

When Iztac reached for the boy's wings, the girl's eyes opened.

Blinding light shot from Kasey, slaying the demon.

"It worked!" Kalen leapt with glee. "Can we do it again?"

***Jodi Jensen** grew up moving from California, to Massachusetts, and a few other places in between, before finally settling in Utah at the ripe old age of nine. The nomadic life fed her sense of adventure as a child and the wanderlust continues to this day. With a passion for old cemeteries, historical buildings and sweeping sagas of days gone by, it was only natural she'd dream of time traveling to all the places that sparked her imagination.*

# The Experiment
## by Alanah Andrews

Bright lights. Blinding. Pressing against my retina.

Pain—all-consuming. A shuddering, piercing, burning pain that dulls occasionally to an ache.

A voice cutting through the pain. "Hello? Can you speak?"

Forcing eyelids open against the glaring lights. Licking cracked lips. "Yes."

A whoop of joy, followed by a soft touch on my hand, pulling me up, up out of my sanctuary.

I can see. A man in a white coat, spattered with a redness that makes me uneasy. Everything aches. He walks behind me, running a hand unnervingly across my back.

"I did it," he breathes. "I created an angel."

*Alanah Andrews* writes speculative fiction and spends far too much time debating whether 1984 or The Handmaid's Tale are most representative of our future. Her YA dystopian novel about a future where emotions are forbidden, Eve of Eridu, was released in 2018. She has also had several short stories published in a range of different places. When she's not writing, Alanah runs the Australian Speculative Fiction group, teaches high school English, and attempts to raise two children. She has a husky, a pony, a blue-tongue lizard, and dreams of travelling Australia in a bus.
Website: www.alanahandrews.com
Facebook: alanahandrewsauthor

# Final Battle
## by C.L. Williams

After centuries of war between the angels of heaven and the demons of hell, it is time to end this once and for all.

Judgement Day is now upon us.

The final war to determine the fate of humanity is now here.

God called for all of his angels while Satan called for all of his demons.

The war, unlike any war ever fought, is too evenly matched. For every angel that's destroyed, a demon is destroyed. No side is truly stronger than the other, but there must be a winner. They continue to fight until a winner is made.

*C.L. Williams is an independent author from central Virginia. He has written eight poetry books, four novellas, one novel, and a contributor to multiple anthologies, with the most recent appearance being an all-ages anthology titled Temoli from Thazbook. His most recent poetry book, The Paradox Complex, features the poem "Sad Crying Clown" that is now a video on YouTube directed by Matthew Mark Hunter of MMH Productions. C.L. Williams is currently working on his first sci-fi book, an all-ages book titled Novo: Away from Earth. When not writing, C.L. Williams is reading and sharing the work of other independent authors.*
*Facebook: writer434*
*Twitter: @writer_434*

# The Sin of Repentance
## by Aiki Flinthart

My fiery sword lay at the woman's throat, but she raised her bruised face and glared.

"Repent," I said. "For you have sinned and may not enter."

"I'll not." She twisted her bloodied, torn shift in both hands and brandished it. "Those that used me thus deserved death at my blade. Where are they, now?" She craned to see beyond.

"They repented and have passed through the Gate."

Her swollen eyes glittered. Her split lip curled in a sneer. She spat.

"Then I want no part of it."

"Your words condemn you." My sword impaled her. Flames absorbed her screams.

*Aiki Flinthart has had short stories shortlisted in the Aurealis awards and top-8 listed in the USA Writers of the Future competition, as well as published in various anthologies and e-mags. She has 11 published spec fic novels and has edited 2 short story anthologies. She regularly gives workshops on writing fight scenes at conventions. Lives in Brisbane. Does martial arts, archery, knife throwing and lute-playing.*
*Website: www.aikiflinthart.com*

# A Soldier's Honour
## by David Bowmore

We were separated from our battalion and had wandered for half a day, until a French girl gave us sanctuary in her father's farmhouse for the night.

It was the way my comrade looked at her out of the corner of his eye, as she laid bread and cheese before us, which alarmed me.

She wouldn't be safe while we remained under her roof.

Hearing him creep from the room we shared, I followed. Whatever innocence our merciful angel had, was about to be lost forever.

He died quickly, before harm was done.

Then she pointed the pistol at me.

*David Bowmore has lived here, there and everywhere, but now lives in Yorkshire with his wonderful wife and a small white poodle. He has worn many hats in his time; head chef, teacher and landscape gardener. His first collection of short stories 'The Magic of Deben Market' is available from Clarendon House.*
*Website: davidbowmore.co.uk*
*Facebook: davidbowmoreauthor*

# The Devil's Playground
by Melissa Neubert

He stood looking out over his kingdom, admiring his underworld.

Fires burned, illuminating the darkness. Cages held the unredeemable, those who committed the ultimate sins during their time on earth. They begged, screamed, and bargained. It did them no good. They were now his to do what he did best; torture.

The shadows brought the newcomers daily. He always wondered why they didn't learn. Earthly monsters committed murder and rape, they tortured children. They had to know what the future held for them.

He smiled at the thought that would get what they deserved as he called his hell hounds.

*Melissa Neubert was born in the Pacific Northwest and currently lives in Illinois with her husband, three children and two dogs. Melissa has been a daycare provider, veterinary assistant, teacher/library aide, and administrative assistant. Melissa travels extensively both domestically and internationally where she finds inspiration for her writing in beautiful and unique locations. When she is not writing she enjoys music, reading, concert and wildlife photography, football and camping. Although Melissa has been writing since grade school, she has only recently begun pursuing the craft seriously. She writes mostly in the genres of Suspense/Thriller and Adult Paranormal Romance.*

# Recruiting
## by Raven Corinn Carluk

"Another one destroyed, My Lord." David knelt, hands clasped in prayer, eyes locked on the angel statue above the altar. "One more sinful soul released from this plane."

The angel's voice reverberated in his heart. *You have done well, my servant.*

"Anything for you."

*Did you allow him a chance to repent?*

"Of course not. Find the sinner. Kill them. Send them straight to Hell." His fervour caused him to shake.

The angel's laughter echoed through the church. *My army is nearly complete, and they never noticed me building it.*

"Your plan was genius, Lord Lucifer. Praise be your name."

*Raven Corinn Carluk is an indie author of dark fantasy and paranormal romance.*
*Website: RavenCorinnCarluk.Blogspot.Com*

# Lucky
## by Andreas Hort

"Scream and I'll cut your throat," growled the man with the knife.

Anna looked around for help, but tonight the street was deserted.

A white flash of bright light appeared, lifting the man off his feet and hurling him against a wall. He collapsed on the sidewalk, unconscious.

Anna squinted at the shining form in front of her and recognised it.

"Lucky?"

Her childhood dog wagged his tail and barked cheerfully. She made out a pair of wings on his back. He spread them and flew up into the night sky.

She turned around and walked home, smiling. Feeling safe.

*Andreas Hort resides in a small town in the northern part of the Czech Republic. When he is not earning his daily bread working various, usually physically oriented jobs, he writes and takes steps toward his goal to move to an English-speaking country. He was never published in English before. In his free time, he works out, studies the investment business, and, of course, reads.*
*Facebook: andreas.hort.71*
*Twitter: @Ondrej_Hort*

# Father Angelo
## by Derek Dunn

"Help!"

It was a whisper, but the cry of urgency pierced Father Angelo's soul. He hurried down the darkened street, searching for a sign. He'd heard the voices before. The angels had led him to many a poor and suffering man. It was his life's mission. So, when the voices called, he listened. Only this one was different.

"Father, please come in," said a frail voice from within a door.

He followed and smiled at the old man as he entered. The door slammed shut, but the man was gone.

Then, a warning from a more familiar voice: "Get out!"

*Derek Dunn lives in the American Northwest with his family. He's a film enthusiast and musician who writes primarily horror and mystery stories.*
*Twitter: @DerekTDunn*

# Thunder
## by D.M. Burdett

Thunder roars as I wait, the last of me soaking into the muddied battlefield, and the war rages on around me, deafening and vicious.

My final breaths ache and burn, and I know my time is soon. I peer longingly across the misty field watching for the Valkyries that will surely come to take me to Valhalla; I have lain my life for Odin, for Ragnarok.

But my pain gives way to a single betraying tear and then Freyja comes to me, beckons.

*I am not for Folkvangr! Go away!*

How can a single tear forsake my life, my sacrifice?

*D.M. Burdett initially roamed as an army brat, but now lives in Australia where she spends her days avoiding drop bears and killer spiders. She has published a Sci-Fi series, has short stories in various anthologies, and has published two children's series. She is currently working on the first book in a dystopian series.*
*Website: www.dmburdett.com*
*Facebook: DMBurdett*

# Morality
by C.L. Williams

I am left with a moral decision to make; an angel appears atop of my left shoulder.

"Lead not into temptation," he says as he warns me of the decision I'm about to make. After he finishes, the antithesis of what's on my left shoulder appears sitting on my right shoulder.

"Screw them, do what's best for you!"

I hear the two of them argue about what's best for me. I ultimately choose to make the decision suggested by the one on my right. He then kills the angel on my left shoulder, and we go through with the decision.

*C.L. Williams is an independent author from central Virginia. He has written eight poetry books, four novellas, one novel, and a contributor to multiple anthologies, with the most recent appearance being an all-ages anthology titled Temoli from Thazbook. His most recent poetry book, The Paradox Complex, features the poem "Sad Crying Clown" that is now a video on YouTube directed by Matthew Mark Hunter of MMH Productions. C.L. Williams is currently working on his first sci-fi book, an all-ages book titled Novo: Away from Earth. When not writing, C.L. Williams is reading and sharing the work of other independent authors.*
*Facebook: writer434*
*Twitter: @writer_434*

# Feathers
## by Alanna Robertson-Webb

I used to think that the iridescent feathers I found were from ravens or crows, but now I know better. My guardian angel is sick, and his beautiful wings are moulting.

I used to think that I was a good person, until I learned that my actions caused his wings to darken, and his halo to tarnish. Now I have a letter sitting on my desk, and it didn't come from any human.

I used to think that I was redeemable, until he died last night. Now there's no salvation for me, and my new demon is on his way.

*Alanna Robertson-Webb is a sales support member by day, and a writer and editor by night. She loves VT, and live in PA. She has been writing since she was five years old, and writing well since she was seventeen years old. She lives with a fiance and a cat, both of whom take up most of her bed space. She loves to L.A.R.P., and one day she aspired to write a horrifyingly fantastic novel. Her short horror stories have been published before, but she still enjoys remaining mysterious.*
*Reddit: MythologyLovesHorror*

# First Revenge
## by Shawn M. Klimek

The winged figure who greeted Cherise in the afterlife broke the news that she had been worshipping the wrong god all along but could redeem herself by serving time as an avenging angel. She readily agreed.

"I would like to avenge myself first on that oafish commuter who knocked me off the subway platform," she declared.

"Impossible," said the greeter. "He is already dead."

Cherise was astonished. "So soon? Was he hit by the same train as me?"

"No," explained the greeter. "He died of pneumonia months ago, because you kicked him off your doorstep. You were his first revenge."

*Shawn M. Klimek is a writer whose other recent anthologies include: "Full Metal Horror 2", by Zombie Pirate Publishing, "Organic Ink" by Dragon Soul Press, "Grumpy Old Gods (Vols. 1 & 2)" by Stormdance Publications, and soon, "Blaze: Inner Circle Writer's Group Flash Fiction Anthology 2019."*
*Website: jotinthedark.blogspot.com*
*Facebook: shawnmklimekauthor*

# Battle Premonition
by William J. Joel

I felt the itch before I saw anything in the mirror. But there they were; two, bright red, vertical ridges on either side of my spine. Within days, my skin would tear, and tiny feathers would emerge.

How long had I been on Earth, waiting? How many humans had I fallen in love with, married, had children with? And in just a few months it would no longer matter. Earth would once again become a battleground, good against evil, or something like that. All I can do is wait for the inevitable.

Maybe this time there might actually be winners.

*All things are connected. That's the premise of what **William J. Joel** does. Each of Mr. Joel's interests informs each other. Mr. Joel has been teaching computer science since 1983 and has been a poet even longer. His poems have appeared in Chronogram, Common Ground Review, and Gravel Magazine.*
*Website: www.aniprof.com*

# The Gateway
## by K.T. Tate

In this chapel I will ascend.

Drawing the symbols with red-stained hands, I speak the divine prayers. My tongue scars as angelic language spills forth. Celestial symbols materialise, burning into my flesh, creating hallowed ground. I am blessed with glorious purpose, weightless and blinded by heavenly light.

Weeping in the presence of such deific beauty I feel something in me crack, unfurling me from chin to crotch. Hands of blazing light push out from me, reaching for existence. Everything I am burns away in rapturous transcendence.

*I am left undone, not a saint but a gateway for the angels.*

***K.T. Tate*** *lives in Cambridgeshire in the UK. She writes mainly weird fiction, cosmic horror and strange monster stories.*
*Website: eldritchhollow.wordpress.com*
*Tumblr: eldritch-hollow.tumblr.com*

# Guiding Vision
## by Dawn DeBraal

Every night, Emily prayed she'd find her missing child.

The news no longer carried the story. Posters of her daughter—tacked on buildings and lampposts—had faded.

The only thing keeping Emily alive was the possibility of her daughter's safe return.

A vision appearing in the form of an angel beckoned Emily to come. Emily didn't hesitate, following closely. The angel stopped, pointing to the small basement window of her neighbour's house, then she disappeared.

Emily didn't care; breaking the window, she climbed down into the basement. She discovered her daughter locked away in a room. Scared but still alive.

*Dawn DeBraal lives in rural Wisconsin with her husband, two rat terriers, and a cat. She successfully raised two children (meaning they didn't return to the nest!) After many years serving the government at the Federal and County level, she recently retired. Having extra time on her hands she started to write after a paralyzed vocal cord took her ability to speak for two months. Not finding her voice, she discovered that her love of telling a good story could be written. Her works have been published in Palm-Sized Press, Spillwords, Mercurial Stories, Potato Soup Journal, and Blood Song Books.*

# The Fall of Heaven
## by Michael Kellichner

Nostrils filled with the smoke of her burning city, the angel passed through amethyst doors and descended into darkness. The old guards of feathers and light had all gone to defend and left the corridors empty except whispers from the imprisoned. Running, feet slapping hollow echos through places taught never to go; the slat in the door of unbreakable metal to see the demon of carmine and melanite, exuding fire and motionless like a mountain.

"So?" the demon in chains said. Smirked. "Will you release me to save all that you love?"

The angel, too young, too afraid, said, "Yes."

*Michael Kellichner is a writer and poet from Pennsylvania currently living in South Korea. Other short fiction of his has been published in Black Denim Lit, Trigger Warnings: Short Fiction with Pictures, and Three Crows Magazine. Twitter: @mithalanis*

# Devil Trap
## by Matt Lucas

All my life the devil's chased me. His poisoned breath seared my neck and his noxious stench filled my nostrils. He lurked in shadow, just out of view, reaching for me with jagged claws.

He pursued me through a wilderness. Oppressed and barren, I mourned my tortured existence. Until one night, a prayer for salvation, revealed a new path.

At the end of the pathway stood a being cloaked in pure light. His brilliance was so majestic, I dared not look upon his face. Light eradicated the shadow beast, sealing my liberation. The devil had chased me into God's arms.

*Matt Lucas is a drone, who still remembers life before corporate mind control. Desperately, his soul yearns to burst forth from his cubicle- shaped imprisonment and write riveting fiction wrought with action and twists. Now, having secured an agent and actively pitching for publication, he's undertaking submitting to smaller publication to gauge interest in new ideas in sci-fi, fantasy, and other genres. Writing is his passion and he hopes to spend his days cultivating captivating stories with impactful messages.*

# On the Nature of Angelic Beings
by Roxanne Dent

We archangels, seraphs, cherubim and guardians are as diverse as the leaves on trees, or grains of sand. Some seek to advance the human race and protect the planet. Others, spiteful and jealous. We number in the thousands and are divided in our battle for control of earth.

I've watched as members of my race plant malicious seeds into human minds. Wars erupt, rape and murder increase, greed escalates. Earth is our playground. Humanity is the game we play as one side wins and the other loses.

One day, we may wipe out humanity for the sake of the game.

*Roxanne Dent has sold nine novels and dozens of short stories in a variety of genres including Paranormal Fantasy, Regency, Mystery, Horror and YA. She has also co-authored short stories and plays with her sister, Karen Dent. Member of New England Horror Writers, The Fiction Writers Guild, Berlin Writers Group, Essex Writers and Artists Group.*

# Thief in the Night
## by Zoey Xolton

Lailah, the angel of conception and childbirth, plucked a soul from the Garden of Eden, setting it within the mother's womb to grow. As the months went by, Lailah ensured the child's wellbeing.

In the night, Lilith, the Outcast, a demoness of infertility and child loss, came. With taloned fingers she raked at the expectant mother's womb. Blood flowed, and the mother wept. The following day the infant was stillborn, and Lailah held the grieving mother.

Lilith stole the child's soul, nursing it with her hate. "Hush, little one," she cooed. "Life is a beautiful lie, but death is eternal!"

*Zoey Xolton is an Australian Speculative Fiction writer, primarily of Dark Fantasy, Paranormal Romance and Horror. She is also a proud mother of two and is married to her soul mate. Outside of her family, writing is her greatest passion. She is especially fond of short fiction and is working on releasing her own themed collections in future.*
*Website: www.zoeyxolton.com*

# That They Should Have Wings
## by Terry Miller

Someone once told me that when we die, we become angels. I dreamt of walking in the clouds, of streets of gold, and flying through the heavens. Well, I never got my wings. My feet never walked on gold nor clouds, not here. Here they watched you through coal-black stares, their gaze penetrating and chilling. You cannot hide your sins, they find you; each and every fault. They observe through the cocoon of their dark wings, as if to protect themselves from the soul filth. The fallen angels. How were they less guilty than us, that they should have wings?

*Terry Miller* is an author and 2017 Rhysling Award-nominated poet residing in Portsmouth, OH, USA. He has self-published a dark poetry collection on Amazon and one short story to date. His work has also appeared in Sanitarium, Devolution Z, Jitter Press, Poetry Quarterly, O Unholy Night in Deathlehem, and the 2017 Rhysling Anthology from the Science Fiction and Fantasy Poetry Association.
Facebook: tmiller2015

# Gospel Truth
## by Joel R. Hunt

Gabriel tucked in his wings as he sat down, slamming three glasses of ambrosia onto the table.

"Right," he said, "Father's down on Earth, so let's get to the good stuff: What's the most evil thing you've ever done? I'll start. Sometimes I visit random humans and tell them they're the Messiah, just to mess with their heads."

"That's nothing," said Raphael, "I once broke the Seventh Seal, glued it back together and never told anyone."

Gabriel roared and hammered the table.

"Brilliant!" he cried, "What about you Michael?"

Michael took a sip of ambrosia and smiled.

"I framed Satan."

*Joel R. Hunt is a writer from the UK who dabbles in the darker aspects of life, particularly through horror, science fiction and the supernatural. He has been published here and there (though likely nowhere you've heard of) and hopes to have released his first anthology of short stories later this year.*
*Twitter: @JoelRHunt1*
*Reddit: JRHEvilInc*

# ANGELS

## ACKNOWLEDGEMENTS

Once again, we have loved reading every single one of the drabbles submitted to the ANGELS anthology; the second in the DARK DRABBLES series. The wealth of talent we are seeing every day is just astounding. So, to everyone who took the time to craft a tiny tale just for us; we thank you from the bottom of our hearts.

And, to everyone who has helped us with this project—families, friends, collaborators, and random strangers who took pity on us—we couldn't have done it without you.

We thank and love you all.

May angels forever watch over you.

www.blackharepress.com

Beatific angels, holy wars, kitty saviours, epic battles between good and evil, devils and demons, fallen angels and many more tantalising tiny tales.

Available 23rd July 2019

Wendigos, vampires, things that go bump in the night or hide under the bed, witches, demons, upirs, kelpies, toad people, zombies, sirens and hundreds of other tiny terrifying tales.

Available 20th August 2019

Micro myths of the paranormal;
poltergeists, spirit boards, ghosts
and ghouls, avenging apparitions
and horrifying hauntings.

Available 3rd September 2019